MYSTERIES *of* **MARTHA'S VINEYARD**

A Light in the Darkness
Like a Fish Out of Water
Adrift
Maiden of the Mist
Making Waves
Don't Rock the Boat
A Port in the Storm
Thicker Than Water

MYSTERIES *of* MARTHA'S VINEYARD

Thicker
Than
Water

DeANNA JULIE DODSON

Guideposts
New York

Cover and interior design by Müllerhaus
Cover illustration by Greg Copeland, represented by Deborah Wolfe, LTD.
Typeset by Aptara, Inc.

Printed and bound in the United States of America
10 9 8 7 6 5 4 3 2 1

CHAPTER ONE

Priscilla Grant huddled under her driftwood-gray afghan in front of the living room's blazing hearth fire, warming her hands around a cup of hot coffee. Along with this cottage, she had inherited the Misty Harbor Lighthouse from her aunt Marjorie Latham, and she had been working hard the past few weeks on the small museum she was creating on the lighthouse's bottom floor, a tribute to the Latham branch of the family and to the old lighthouse itself. For today, though, she was taking a break. It would be nice just to putter around the house for a while, read, maybe work on her long-neglected appliqué quilt. One thing was certain, she wasn't going out in the cold March drizzle on foot again today. As much as she and Jake enjoyed brisk walks all year long, she was sure he was glad to be back inside the cozy cottage now too.

She smiled at her dog as he lay snoozing in front of the fire. Though he was almost two years old now, he was often still like a puppy with only two gears: full speed ahead and full stop. He didn't even twitch when her cell phone rang.

"Have you heard?" Trudy said before Priscilla could say hello. "Have you heard what's going on?"

Trudy was one of the three cousins Priscilla had become close to since moving to Martha's Vineyard. Unlike Priscilla, her cousins were natives of the island, and they were consequently rather protective of it and its history.

"Hi, Trudy," Priscilla said, hearing in her cousin's voice only her usual excitability and nothing to indicate a life-threatening emergency. "Have I heard what?"

"Caroline Waterman is selling!"

Priscilla had heard of the Watermans. They owned acres of valuable land that had so far been left untouched, much to the satisfaction of the island's residents. Priscilla had heard much speculation, which had evidently been going on for decades, about what it would take to convince Miss Waterman to sell, why she was so dead set against it, and what her mostly absent relations would do when she passed away.

Once Miss Waterman had surpassed the age of eighty, people finally began to believe she was serious when she said she wanted to leave the land in its natural state for as long as possible, at least during her lifetime. But now—

"Are you sure?" Priscilla asked. "I thought—"

"We all thought!" Trudy almost always talked in exclamation points. "She's closing the museum too, and selling off all the artifacts and memorabilia."

"Oh, not really. That's too bad."

Despite living on Martha's Vineyard for several months, Priscilla still hadn't had a chance to visit the Cavanaugh Museum. It was a bit of an oddity. Not too different, she supposed, from the little Latham family museum she was planning, though the Cavanaughs were certainly better known and much more controversial than any of the Lathams had ever been.

"How did you find out?" she asked Trudy. "It's not already a done deal, is it?"

"I ran into Mildred at Ortmann's when I went to get vegetables to make stew for dinner. She's just sure that land's going to be crammed full of McMansions within a month or two!"

"I don't think they can do anything like that so fast."

"Well, that's what she thinks!"

"Wouldn't that kind of development have to be approved by—"

"Oh, you know how it is. People with enough money can do whatever they want. I just hate to see that part of the island spoiled that way."

"What else did Mildred say?" Priscilla asked. "Did she know who—"

"Nothing like that yet. It's only just come out!"

"Well, whatever actually happens, it's Miss Waterman's land. There's not a lot we can do about it if she wants to sell."

Trudy sighed in defeat. "I suppose you're right. But it seems like such a shame. I think Mildred was much more upset about losing the museum than anything else."

"It could be that whoever buys the contents will display them in a different location," Priscilla said. "Maybe in Boston at some of the other historical sites."

4 | MYSTERIES of MARTHA'S VINEYARD

"You know I don't know anything about old stuff. But I do wish I had some of the clothes Rosie Cavanaugh had back in the forties. That woman knew how to dress."

"I suppose she had to if she was going to marry into that family and be on display all the time." Priscilla laughed softly. "Not for me, thank you very much."

"Well, I don't suppose either of us will ever have that problem," Trudy said, her voice wistful. "Anyhow, I'd better go. This stew is one of those Crock-Pot recipes that take all day to cook, and if I don't get it started, Dan and I won't eat till midnight. I just thought you ought to know about Miss Waterman, especially since Joan and Gail are both at work and can't talk right now."

"We'll have a chat about it the next time the four of us are together," Priscilla promised. "Maybe there's nothing to the story after all."

"Maybe." Trudy didn't sound at all convinced. "Hey, you haven't forgotten Joan's birthday, have you?"

"Of course not. I've been counting the days. I found the most perfect present for her. I can't wait till she sees it."

"Ooh! What? What?"

"Oh, no," Priscilla said. "I heard that Joan told you what she was giving Gail for Christmas a couple of years ago, and everybody on Martha's Vineyard knew what it was by the middle of December, including Gail."

"Fine," Trudy huffed. "One little mistake..."

Priscilla laughed. "You'd better get back to your stew. I'll talk to you later."

Once she had ended the call, Priscilla picked up her coffee cup again and breathed in the dark, rich aroma, but she didn't feel cold anymore. She had too much to think about right now. Jake was still asleep on the braided rag rug on the hearth, but she decided maybe she would go out again after all.

A few minutes later, she put on her coat and headed out to the Cavanaugh Museum. She had been meaning to go anyway, if just to get a few ideas about how to organize her own displays, and it wouldn't do for it to close before she ever got to see it.

She didn't know much about the Cavanaughs, only that the family had made their money out West in the last part of the nineteenth century and then had come east to settle down respectably. Since then, their wealth and influence had grown until they were well known not only in Martha's Vineyard but nationally and globally. Priscilla didn't want to miss her chance to get an up-close look at whatever was on display, especially if it was going to be her last.

Cavanaugh Museum House wasn't all that large, but it was a lovely three-story Victorian with towers and turrets, gingerbread trim, stained-glass windows, and wraparound porches in enough profusion to ensure it was the grandest home of its day. Priscilla scolded herself for not looking up the museum's open hours ahead of time, but there was a green Acura parked in the drive that led to the carriage house, so with luck someone was there to let her in. She had thought there would be other people wanting a tour of the museum, but she saw no other cars. Still, it was midmorning on a cold, drizzly Wednesday in March. Probably not their peak time.

Not quite sure what to do, she tapped on the front door and waited. According to the sign on the door, the museum had been open for over an hour already, so after a moment, she let herself in.

"Hello?"

The foyer was well lit and lined with photographs, some of them only tintypes, others very recent. Some of them were of people she recognized. Others she couldn't possibly identify. As she read the captions, she was more and more amazed by the sheer number of celebrities the various Cavanaughs had rubbed elbows with. Actors and actresses, presidents and kings, politicians, popes and philanthropists, mobsters, scientists, poets and soldiers, activists and revolutionaries. It was quite a gallery, and she had only just stepped inside the door.

"Hello?" she said again, and she heard a door close in another part of the house. Then she heard rapid footsteps, and a door into the main parlor opened.

"Good morning."

The man who greeted her looked to be in his fifties, maybe three or four years younger than Priscilla. His smile was polite, but the eyes behind his thick glasses were rather impatient, as if she had interrupted something he was in a hurry to get done.

"Good morning," she said with a bright smile. "I hope it's all right for me to come in. The sign—"

"Oh, yes, we're open. For now, at least."

She added a touch of sympathy to her smile. "I heard Miss Waterman might be closing this place. What a shame."

His slumped shoulders slumped even more. "Aunt Caroline is being very difficult, if you'll excuse my saying so."

Priscilla's eyebrows went up. "She's your aunt?"

"For all the good that does. We haven't really spoken for over twenty years, and now she won't see me at all." He made a sour face. "I'm Malcolm Waterman. My father was her brother, but I suppose I shouldn't bore you with my family when it's the Cavanaughs you've come to learn about. Well, it's a good thing you didn't wait too long to visit." He made a sweeping gesture with both thin arms, encompassing the parlor. "Help yourself. Or would you rather have the guided tour?"

"I'm sure there's a lot you could tell me about everything." She couldn't help wondering about this falling-out between him and his aunt, even though it was none of her business. As she hoped, he followed her over to the first of the display cases. It was full of medals from conflicts throughout the world, from the Spanish-American War in 1898 to Afghanistan over a hundred years later. All of them had been awarded to Cavanaughs.

"Pretty amazing, huh?" he asked, looking over the display. "You know, I used to hate this place. I wanted Aunt Caroline to close it. But recently I've come to appreciate everything here. It's an incredible collection. A microcosm of twentieth-century America."

"It is that," she said, strolling from the medals to the display of an elegant white silk dress with handmade Irish lace and seed pearls and, if the placard was to be believed, a twelve-foot train.

Displayed with it was a gorgeous lace veil and dainty silk slippers. The celebrated beauty Rosalie Millican West, daughter of Texas oil magnate Bronson West, had worn the dress when she was married to Rowan Neville Cavanaugh II on June 18, 1941.

"I'm curious," Priscilla said. "How did your aunt Caroline get all these things? I would have thought the Cavanaugh family would want to keep them."

"Many of the items are just on loan. Some of them have been donated or sold to the museum by the Cavanaughs or friends of theirs, by collectors, even by other museums. Mostly we have them because my father asked the family for objects to display when he decided to open the museum in '52. Samuel Cavanaugh moved his family into this house when they came here in 1875, but they built that big place up-island in the late forties, so Dad bought this house and made it a museum. Old Sam and my great-great-grand-father Elias Waterman made a lot of money in San Francisco during those Wild West days. I won't admit exactly how, but the Watermans and the Cavanaughs have been great friends ever since. Well, not that we run in the same circles anymore, of course, not after they went into politics and war *hero-ing* and all that. But yeah, everything here has a pretty interesting story."

She looked at him, not sure if she should be amused or surprised by his casual admissions. "I don't suppose this is what you usually tell your visitors."

He shrugged. "Does it matter anymore?"

"Are you sure your aunt won't discuss her decision with you? If I were to guess, I'd say a lot of people on the island will be unhappy if she sells her land, and many others would like to see this museum stay open. Maybe someone in her family could—"

"Not me, thank you, if that's what you're getting at. She lets her lawyer contact me if there's something I need to know. Last time I tried to talk to her, her housekeeper threatened to set the dog on me."

Priscilla bit her lip, suppressing the urge to find out more. Instead, she had him show her the rest of the museum that documented the lives and accomplishments of six generations of Cavanaughs. As he had said, it really was a microcosm of twentieth-century America.

"I'll have to come back sometime," she told him as they reached the entryway again. "There's so much to see and study."

"Better not wait too long," he said, and with a cynical smirk, he shut the door behind her.

Priscilla decided to stop by the bakery on her way home. She didn't know whether she would just pick up her usual cranberry muffin and chocolate chip cookies or actually stay and eat something a little fancier. It would depend on what was written on the chalkboard menu for the day's specials.

"Hi, Candy," Priscilla said as she approached the counter. She was met with a bright-eyed smile.

"Priscilla. How are you this morning?"

"Good. I was just over at the Cavanaugh Museum, and I thought I'd stop by for a treat."

The bakery was empty except for a woman in her fifties sitting near the windows that overlooked the harbor. She had looked up from the cream puff she was eating when Priscilla came in, and she was still looking now, frowning slightly.

"I suppose you've heard it might be closing," Priscilla said, turning away from the other woman and back to Candy.

"Yes." Candy shook her head. "Such a shame. I didn't think Miss Waterman—"

"Excuse me." The woman at the table stood up, smiling apologetically as she approached Priscilla. "I'm so sorry to interrupt, and I didn't mean to be eavesdropping, but aren't you Priscilla Grant?"

Priscilla stared at her for a moment and then rushed to hug her. "Kitty! Oh my goodness, Kitty! What are you doing here?"

"What are *you* doing here? You can't have left the farm."

"I can," Priscilla assured her, "and I have."

Kitty shook her head, her brown eyes warm in her plump face. "I never thought you'd be able to pry Gary away from the place."

"I'm afraid I lost Gary to cancer over a year ago."

Kitty's smile faded. "Oh, Priscilla, I'm so sorry. I had no idea."

"It's all right." Priscilla swallowed an unexpected lump in her throat and gave Kitty a wry grin. "Most days." She looked at Candy. "This is an old school friend of mine from Kansas, Kitty Merrick. We haven't seen each other in at least fifteen years."

"Twenty," Kitty said.

"Well, it sounds like the two of you have some catching up to do over coffee and chocolate chip cookies," Candy told them. "My treat."

They thanked her and went back to Kitty's table, both of them in a hurry to catch up on the past twenty-plus years.

"But why are *you* here?" Priscilla asked once she had told Kitty about inheriting the cottage and the lighthouse. "You don't live in the area, do you?"

"Oh, no. After we left Wheatfield, Keith and I moved to Oregon. I'm here on a business trip."

"Really? Are you still in real estate?"

"Not residential anymore, no. I know nobody from Kansas would believe I have the personality for it, but I do big commercial deals now."

"Nice," Priscilla said, taking a bite of her cookie, and then she frowned a little. "You're not involved in the sale of all that land over past Oak Bluffs are you?"

"Oh, no. My business trip was in Boston, but since I was so close, I thought I'd come over to Martha's Vineyard and catch up with my aunt Katherine."

"I didn't know you had an Aunt Katherine."

"I haven't really kept in touch with her," Kitty admitted. "She was married to my mother's brother, Uncle Bert, but he died in a plane crash on the day I was born. After that, Katherine lived at our house and took care of me while Mom worked. She and Mom were great friends even after Aunt Katherine married again and moved out here. They wrote each other all the time, and after Mom died,

I started writing to her too. Not as much, just a few times a year, but it's been nice getting real cards and letters once in a while."

"That is nice." Priscilla sipped her coffee, still delighted to have a chance to chat with her old friend again. "Does she know you're coming?"

"Well, that's the problem. Or, I should say, that's why I came. Like I said, we haven't written much. Mostly birthday and Christmas cards or a letter here and there when something exciting happens, but I haven't heard from her in five months. Not at Christmas. Not for my birthday in February or hers in March."

Priscilla frowned. "Couldn't you have called her?"

"I don't have a number for her," Kitty said with a sigh. "Just an address. When I tried to get a phone number for the address, all I could find out was that it was unlisted. So I thought, since I had to come out this way anyway, I'd make sure she's all right." There was concern now in her dark eyes. "She's pretty old, and I'm afraid she might have just passed away."

"I guess that's possible," Priscilla said gently. "But that ought to be easy enough to find out, right?"

"I think so. I just got in, so I haven't really gotten started yet. I thought I'd find the address where I'd been writing to her and see what they can tell me."

"Good idea. Want me to help you find the place?"

"That would be great." Kitty fished in her purse for a moment and then brought out an envelope. "Here's the address."

Priscilla looked at it and frowned. If she wasn't mistaken, she was looking at the address of Caroline Waterman's home.

CHAPTER TWO

The Waterman House had been built in 1948, a white clap-board house, broad and long, in the middle of similar homes in its very exclusive neighborhood. The neighborhood was still exclusive, even though it wasn't far from Joan's modest cottage. Trudy had pointed out the house once when she and Priscilla happened to drive by, and Priscilla had been impressed by the pristine condition of the home and lawn and the elegance of its simple lines.

Kitty looked up at it uncertainly and then back at the envelope she had clutched in one hand. "Are you sure this is the right place?"

"This is it," Priscilla assured her. "This is the address you've been writing to. What I don't understand is why your aunt had you address your letters to Miss Waterman instead of to her."

"I thought it was a little odd, but Aunt Katherine said there was someone else in the neighborhood with a name very similar to hers, and she was tired of having to sort things out all the time. And she said everyone knows where Miss Waterman lives."

"That's true," Priscilla said with a chuckle. "I guess it can get confusing for the post office when people have staff living in. Not that I have that problem to deal with."

"You'd think they'd have figured it out after she'd worked for Miss Waterman for fifty years." Kitty looked again at the envelope and then toward the house. "So...do you think it's okay for us to go to the front door and ask for Aunt Katherine? Or should we go around back?"

Priscilla turned off the SUV's engine and unbuckled her seat belt. "I guess if they want us to go around back, they can tell us at the front door."

Kitty smiled tentatively, and they both got out of the car. The front lawn was big, and the shrubbery-lined walkway was long. By the time they got to the door, Priscilla felt as uncertain as Kitty looked. People didn't just walk up to Miss Caroline Waterman's house, did they?

The instant Kitty rang the doorbell, a dog started barking inside the house. A big dog, Priscilla knew at once, deep-chested and snarling. She wasn't surprised when she noticed the Beware of Dog sign posted by the door. It was right under the one that said No Solicitors.

"Should I ring again?" Kitty asked a couple of minutes later when no one had come to the door. "Maybe no one's home."

"I haven't lived on the island very long," Priscilla said, trying to see through the blinds of the narrow windows on either side of the door without being obvious, "but even I know Caroline Waterman never leaves home. Someone's got to be here. And I can't imagine she'd answer the door herself."

The sound of barking rushed closer, and there was a thud of large paws against the door.

"Down," snapped a harsh voice from inside. "Down. Quiet."

The dog yelped, and then there was silence.

Kitty looked at Priscilla, wide-eyed. "Maybe—"

The door opened, and a tall, rawboned woman with short blonde hair and diamond earrings peered out. "Yes?"

Kitty swallowed hard, evidently too nervous to say anything.

Priscilla managed a smile. "Hello. We're sorry to bother you, but this is Miss Waterman's house, isn't it?"

"We don't receive sales calls," the woman said coldly, and she started to close the door.

"Wait." Kitty grabbed the doorknob. "We're not selling anything. We don't want to bother Miss Waterman. I'm just looking for Katherine Evans."

The woman narrowed her eyes. "Why? Who's she to you?"

"Sh-she's my aunt." Kitty faltered at the woman's obvious suspicion. "She was married to my mother's brother."

"This is the last address she has for her," Priscilla supplied when Kitty looked pleadingly at her. "Is she here? Or could you take a message for her?"

"I'm sorry," the woman said, her expression finally softening. "Ms. Evans passed away before I came to work here."

"Oh." Kitty's shoulders slumped. "I—I see."

"I'm afraid I don't know anything more than that. I'm sorry."

"Thank you for your help," Priscilla said.

"I'm sorry," the woman repeated. "Good afternoon."

Kitty didn't say anything until they were back in the SUV and halfway down the street.

"I was afraid that might be what had happened." She looked down, and a single tear fell onto the envelope she still held. "At least I know now."

"I'm so sorry." Priscilla patted Kitty's hand, keeping her eyes on the road ahead.

"I'm sorry to be so sappy." Kitty passed one hand over her eyes with a sheepish grin. "I don't know why I'm surprised. She was eighty-five, or would have been. I guess that's a good long life in anyone's books."

"I know that's not what you wanted to hear, though. Too bad that woman couldn't tell you anything else about her."

Kitty glanced back toward the house. "I wish we could have talked to Miss Waterman. Aunt Katherine worked for her for such a long time and knew her very well. It would have been nice to hear more about her life here and what her last days were like."

"Caroline Waterman doesn't talk to her own nephew except through her lawyers," Priscilla said, "but I'm sure there are other places to get information. At least we can find out the basic facts, right?"

The Tisbury Town Hall was a multistory white clapboard building with a red-bricked front yard and a tall, church-like steeple. There was a portico over the front door with two stairways leading up to it, one on each side. Priscilla wasn't sure if visitors were allowed to go up there, but she decided to start with the door on the ground floor. Kitty seemed quite willing to follow her lead.

After a few false starts, they found the right department, filled out the request for the death certificate for Katherine Elizabeth Evans, née Martin, and paid the fee. A little while later, the clerk handed Kitty a copy of the certificate. Kitty looked it over, her face growing more and more concerned.

Priscilla couldn't help being concerned too. "What is it?"

"Under cause of death, it says fractured cervical vertebrae and the 'accident' box is checked. She fell down the stairs."

Priscilla put her hand over her mouth, covering a gasp. "She broke her neck?"

"I'm sure that's what it means."

"I'm so sorry." Priscilla put her arm around her friend's shoulders and gave her a comforting squeeze. "That's such a shame."

"It makes sense that it would've been an accident. She was always so healthy. I don't remember her ever talking about going to the doctor, even at her age." Kitty rubbed her eyes and smiled faintly. "Well, I guess now I know what happened."

"May I see?" Priscilla asked.

Kitty handed her the certificate, and Priscilla looked it over. It listed a few other details about the death, but the part about the fractured vertebrae was really all they needed to know. Priscilla was about to give the paper back to Kitty, but then she frowned.

"I thought you said she was eighty-four."

Kitty nodded.

"This says she was eighty-two."

Kitty took the death certificate from her. "Well, that's not right. If she died on October 19 last year, she would have been eighty-four. Eighty-five in March. I know because she was the same age as my mother."

"Wait a minute." Priscilla peered at the paper over Kitty's shoulder. "Kitty, this wasn't October 19 of last year. It was two years before that. She would have been eighty-two."

"What?" Kitty shook her head, squinting at the dates typed on the certificate. "They must have gotten the wrong dates. Aunt Katherine's last letter came, I don't know, last fall sometime. It could have been October. Maybe September. I don't have the letter anymore, but I remember writing back to her about my anniversary coming up in November. It had to be before that."

"They probably put in the wrong year of death accidentally and then calculated the age from that," Priscilla said. "We ought to find out how to get it corrected."

She and Kitty went back to the clerk, who told them that only the informant or the coroner could apply to amend the information on a death certificate and that the appropriate form was available online.

Priscilla studied the death certificate as they walked back to the SUV, but she stopped abruptly before she stepped off the curb. "I don't think the informant is going to be any help in this."

Kitty looked at her enquiringly.

"The informant of record," Priscilla said, "is one Caroline Waterman, notorious recluse."

Kitty's forehead wrinkled. "I suppose that makes sense, if she fell at the Waterman house. Aunt Katherine told me it was only the two of them most of the time, besides the cleaning service that took care of the really heavy work. That must have been terrible for Miss Waterman, finding her like that, since they were such friends."

"Were they?"

"Oh, yes. Aunt Katherine didn't have any family once her second husband died, and she said Miss Waterman really didn't either, except that one nephew you mentioned. Aunt Katherine always said Miss Waterman was upset with her whole family because they never paid any attention to her. Never called or visited unless they wanted something. Didn't even send thank-you cards for birthday and Christmas presents. She finally refused to see anyone anymore except her lawyer and Aunt Katherine. It must have been hard to lose her best friend."

"That's so sad." Priscilla looked at the information the clerk had given them. "Do you want to go see the coroner? We can get him to request the correction and won't have to bother Miss Waterman about it. That new housekeeper of hers certainly doesn't encourage visitors."

Kitty bit her lip. "I hate to bother you with this. I'm sure you have a lot of other things you wanted to do with your day."

"Actually, I was taking the day off," Priscilla said with a laugh. "Get in."

Once they were buckled up, she started the engine and guided the SUV into the street.

"Even though you're taking the day off," Kitty said after a moment, "that doesn't mean you don't have plans. I can see to this myself."

"That wouldn't be very hospitable of me, now would it?" Priscilla glanced over at her. "I still don't know everything about Vineyard Haven, but I bet I know more than you do. Read me that address, and we'll get this straightened out. After that, you can come see my lighthouse."

Kitty beamed at her.

Priscilla had expected to visit the coroner's office. She hadn't expected to follow that up with a visit to the police.

"So you're telling me you were getting letters from Katherine Evans for two years after she died?" Officer April Brown looked at Kitty, her expression kind but skeptical. "And you're sure about the dates."

Kitty shrugged. "Not exactly sure, but I know I'm not two years off. I know I got a letter from her last fall. Either September or October. I don't care what the death certificate says, it can't be right."

"What about the coroner?" April pushed a lock of her shoulder-length brown hair behind one ear and turned to Priscilla. "I can see someone making a mistake typing up the certificate. The coroner might even have gotten a date wrong here or there, but not all the dates in all his records. Not the funeral home records too. You did check with them, right?"

Priscilla nodded. "There's no grave. The records show she was cremated and her ashes scattered at sea." She exhaled heavily. "Two years ago last fall."

"But you still got letters," April said, frowning as she looked at Kitty. "That is a puzzle."

"We wanted to talk to Miss Waterman about it," Priscilla told her, "but we figured she wouldn't see us. Is there any way you could talk to her? Or send someone out there? According to the death certificate, she's the one who reported the death. Kitty says there wouldn't likely have been anyone else in the house, so Miss Waterman must have found the body. If somebody could talk to her, I'm sure she'd remember what happened and when."

"I doubt Aunt Katherine had any estate to speak of," Kitty said sadly, "so there wouldn't be any inheritance questions, I don't think. I would guess all she left was whatever clothes she owned, and that would be about it. I know she didn't have a car or a house of her own. Her second husband worked for the Cavanaughs too, so they had their living quarters provided and drove the family cars. I think he died sometime in the sixties, and she never married again. She always told me how nice it was that she didn't have a lot of material things to worry about and that she was very comfortable at Miss Waterman's. She said she lived like a rich woman without any of the worries."

Priscilla smiled at her. "I suppose that would be rather nice, having all the comforts even if they weren't technically yours."

"So she and Miss Waterman got along well?" April asked, her tone very businesslike. "Your aunt never wrote you about any disagreements between the two of them?"

Kitty shook her head. "As far as I could tell, they were the best of friends. They watched old movies on Netflix and played cards and read the same books so they could talk about them. I don't think they did much of anything else, from what Aunt Katherine said. They did cross-stitch, but I don't remember any mention of that more recently. Maybe their eyesight wasn't good enough anymore."

"I've never met Miss Waterman," April said, "but I did see Mrs. Evans around town a time or two. Doing the shopping and that sort of thing, but that was years and years ago. Neither one of them got out much the past few years, from what I heard."

"So, can you go talk to her?" Kitty asked anxiously. "To Miss Waterman? If you could just ask her when Aunt Katherine died. There has to be some mistake in the date. Nothing else makes sense."

"I'll go out there," April said, giving her a reassuring smile. "But I don't have a warrant, so if she refuses to see me, then there's not much else I can do."

"But the letters—"

"Let's see what happens. There may be a simple explanation for all of this. If not, then we'll figure out what to do next."

"Do you think it will be today?" Priscilla asked.

"I can't promise," April said with a glance at her file-covered desk. "If Bill and Ed get back in from their patrol on time, then I'll try. Otherwise, it might be tomorrow or the next day." She turned to Kitty. "You're staying in town?"

"She's staying with me," Priscilla said before Kitty could answer. She pulled out her phone to check her contacts. As she did, she noticed several missed calls, all from her daughter, Rachel. Uh-oh. She was going to hear about this. She scrolled through her contact list. "Is your number the same, Officer Brown?"

April nodded. "I'll get back to you as soon as I know something."

"I can't impose on you like this," Kitty said once they were back in the SUV.

"This isn't going to be straightened out today, you know." Priscilla smiled and pulled out onto the street. "I have a perfectly good spare room. Nothing fancy, but it'll keep the rain off."

"I can get a hotel. Or a bed-and-breakfast or whatever you have around here. I don't—"

"But how would we get caught up with each other after so long? And who would help me pick out the present I have in mind for my cousin's birthday?"

That made Kitty laugh. "I'm sure you couldn't possibly do that yourself. And obviously, if I did help you, I couldn't do so unless I was staying at your house."

"Well, if you don't *want* to..." Priscilla said with a melodramatic sigh that made her friend laugh again.

"Okay, yes, I would love to, actually. I hadn't planned to stay more than the afternoon. I'll have to cancel my flight and let my boss and husband know I'll be gone longer than I thought, so not having to find someplace to stay is a big help. Thank you."

"That's settled, then." Priscilla turned back toward Candy's. "Tell me where you're parked, and then you can follow me back to my house. Then we'll figure out what to do next."

They picked up Kitty's rental car and drove back to the cottage. Priscilla had just finished showing her both the cottage and the lighthouse when her cell phone rang. It was Rachel's ringtone. Priscilla loved her daughter dearly, but Rachel did have a tendency to hover now that Priscilla was "all alone" here on Martha's Vineyard.

Priscilla excused herself to Kitty and answered the phone. "Hello, darling. How are you?"

"Mother! I've been trying to get you all morning. What have you been doing?"

"I've been busy." Priscilla smiled apologetically at her houseguest. "I was going to call you back when I was at home."

Kitty pointed toward her suitcase and then toward the spare room, but Priscilla shook her head and motioned for her to make herself comfortable on the couch.

"You know I worry," Rachel said. "You could have at least texted me you'd call me later."

Priscilla sank into the armchair with a sigh. "I know. I'm sorry. I had some unexpected company, and we were—"

"Who? You know there are all kinds of con men trying to take advantage of lonely elderly women."

That startled a laugh out of Priscilla. "Rachel! I am neither lonely nor elderly."

Kitty put her hand over her mouth to cover a giggle.

"Do you remember Kitty and Keith Merrick?" Priscilla asked her daughter. "Your dad and I were friends with them when you were young."

"Oh, yeah," Rachel said after a moment's pause. "I do a little bit. Mr. Merrick used to make quarters come out of my ears."

"That's him. Anyway, I ran into Kitty at the bakery earlier today, and we've been looking into some family matters for her here. She's going to stay a little while, and I'm going to show her around the island, so don't worry if I don't always pick up the phone, okay?"

"You could call me and tell me when you're going someplace," Rachel said.

"I could," Priscilla replied cheerfully, "but I won't. I'm doing fine here, darling, and you don't have to worry about me."

"Mother—"

"How would you feel if I asked you to do what you're asking of me?"

Silence.

"Uh-huh," Priscilla said. "I didn't think so."

"It's just..." For a moment, Rachel was silent again. "I worry about all the things you get involved with out there, all these mysteries. What if you get mixed up in something really serious? And I don't think you tell me half of what goes on."

Priscilla winced. Rachel was more or less right about that. "How about this? If I don't call you back within twenty-four hours, you can call the Tisbury police and have them track me down. Deal?"

Kitty covered another giggle, and Rachel laughed. "All right, Mom, deal."

"Now," Priscilla said, "was there anything you wanted to talk about, or was this only another checkup?"

"Just wanted to make sure you were all right. You know I wouldn't call if I didn't love you."

"I know, darling. I love you too. Now, you have a good day and don't worry, all right?"

"All right, Mom. Talk to you later."

"Sorry about that," Priscilla told Kitty once she had ended the call.

"Oh, don't be sorry. I wish our two boys would call even half that much."

"Well, boys," Priscilla said, and Kitty nodded. There wasn't much more to be said.

"I shouldn't complain," Kitty said. "They do pretty well, but they both have families of their own, and I know how it is trying to balance things between both sets of grandparents. Drew's mother-in-law—"

The phone rang again, but this time it wasn't Rachel. A quick glance told Priscilla the caller was the Tisbury police department.

CHAPTER THREE

O fficer Brown," Priscilla said after April identified herself. "Does this mean you've had a chance to go out to Miss Waterman's?"

"I did," April said, businesslike as always. "Anna Vaden, the housekeeper, let me know it was quite inconvenient for me to come inside right then since she was doing the floors, but she did grudgingly go up to see if Miss Waterman would see me. She was in bed, feeling a little under the weather, Anna said, but in a chipper mood."

"What did Miss Waterman say?" Priscilla asked as Kitty stood in tense silence beside her, listening in. "You did get to see her, right?"

"I spoke to her for only a couple minutes, but I think what she said really explains everything. Katherine Evans did die on October 19 two years ago."

"But—" Kitty began, and Priscilla held up one hand, urging her to hear what April had to say.

"Miss Waterman said she was the one who kept writing to Mrs. Merrick after Katherine died," April continued. "She told me she and Katherine had both enjoyed Mrs. Merrick's cards and letters over the years, and that she would have felt like she had lost another friend if she'd had to give that up too. So she took over."

Kitty frowned but didn't say anything.

"I guess that makes sense," Priscilla said.

"So that solves that," April told her. "I called up the coroner too, just to assure myself there was nothing unusual about the death. He looked in his file and said it was clearly a case of accidental death, that someone that age suffering that kind of fall doesn't stand much of a chance."

"I suppose not." Priscilla sighed. "Thanks for looking into it for us. We only wanted to figure out what happened."

"Not a problem. You both have a good day."

"I don't know," Kitty said once Priscilla had ended the call. "Those letters seemed so much like Aunt Katherine. The handwriting. Everything."

Priscilla frowned. "They had been friends a long time, right? Miss Waterman and your aunt?"

"Since the sixties, I think, so yeah, a long time. But would Miss Waterman be able to reproduce her handwriting and everything?"

"Hmm," Priscilla said. "Are you sure you would have noticed if it had changed just a little bit? Not enough to stand up to analysis or anything, but just when you got a new letter. You said she didn't write all that often. If you hadn't been expecting it to be different, would you have noticed?"

"Okay, probably not. I assumed—"

"And that would explain why she asked you to address the envelopes to Caroline Waterman. Do you remember when you started doing that?"

Kitty thought for a minute and then sighed. "Probably two or three years ago. I can't exactly remember now, but it might have been around the same time Aunt Katherine died." She clasped her hands in her lap, looking faintly embarrassed. "I guess I don't have to reschedule my flight after all."

"You don't have to," Priscilla said with a grin, "but you could. Is there anything you really have to get back to right away?"

"Well, not for a day or so, anyway. I took care of what I needed to for the business trip, but I have a closing with a particularly fussy client coming up, and I really can't miss that. He's the kind who won't do anything without me to hold his hand. To be honest, I'm way overdue for some vacation, but I guess that'll have to wait. Keith has been trying to get me to take a break for a while now. Of course, I thought we'd do something together, but I suppose we can still do that another time."

"Have you ever been to Martha's Vineyard before?" Priscilla asked. "You really ought to take a look around while you're here."

"Are you sure it wouldn't be too much of an imposition? I know I dropped out of the sky right into the middle of your day."

"It's no imposition at all."

"But your cousin's birthday—"

"I promise you she won't mind if you come along. It's only lunch. And, really, you can help me pick out just the right present.

I know what I want to get, but I won't know which particular one until I look them all over. Besides, Rachel will feel better if I'm not here all by myself."

Kitty shook her head. "I guess it's different for me since I still have Keith. I don't know what my boys would be like if he wasn't there. Probably about as overprotective as your daughter."

"I think our kids forget that we managed to raise them without any major mishaps." Priscilla shrugged. "I don't know, though. I sometimes still wonder if I was out of my mind to move out here without knowing what I was getting into. I was never really on my own before. Not like this."

"From what I can tell you've done all right," Kitty assured her. "And you do have your cousins if you need any help, besides everyone in town being your friend."

Priscilla laughed. "Not everyone. I suppose I've gotten to know a lot of the folks here in Tisbury, though. It does make it feel like home."

Kitty looked at her for a long moment and then smiled. "All right, if you're absolutely sure I won't be in the way, I'd love to stay. Only for a day or two, if it's okay."

"Great. Why don't you get settled in the spare room, and then we can make plans."

The next day, Priscilla stopped her SUV in front of the Waterman house and looked at the front door. "The housekeeper made it pretty clear that Miss Waterman doesn't like visitors. And then there's that dog."

Kitty set her full lips into a determined line. "If she and Aunt Katherine were the friends I think they were, and if she enjoyed getting my cards and letters enough to pretend to be Aunt Katherine, then I don't think it's unreasonable to think she'd like to talk to me. At the very least, I'd like to let her know I wouldn't mind writing to her. She must be awfully lonely if she stays up there by herself all the time, especially now that Aunt Katherine is gone."

"Okay." Priscilla turned off the engine. "But if she still doesn't want to see you, then I think we should probably leave her alone, all right?"

Kitty nodded reluctantly, and they went up to the door. The housekeeper did not look happy to see them again. The dog certainly wasn't. Anna Vaden made sure they saw it this time, an enormous German shepherd with a vicious bark. She made a great show of holding it back.

"We're sorry to bother you again," Kitty told her, keeping a wary eye on the dog. "I was just wondering if Miss Waterman—"

"Look, I told you and the police officer you sent over that Miss Watermen doesn't see anyone anymore. If you need to contact her, I can get you the name and address of her attorney."

Kitty looked at Priscilla and then back at Anna. "Would you just take her a quick note? If she enjoyed writing to me so much that she pretended to be my aunt, don't you think she'd at least want to meet me? For a minute or two?"

The housekeeper shrugged. "It's not my decision to make. It seems like a waste of time and paper to me, but go ahead. I'll take it up to her."

Under the dog's constant watch, Kitty rummaged in her purse and found a piece of paper and a pen. She wrote a few lines, folded the page in half, and passed it through the slightly open door. Anna glanced at it and, with a huff, closed the door. She was back a few minutes later with another note.

Kitty opened it, looked it over, and then refolded it with a sigh. "All right. Well, thank you for asking. We won't bother you again."

"I guess she has your address," Anna said, her expression slightly less stern than it had been. "If she changes her mind."

Kitty nodded, and the housekeeper shut the door. Priscilla and Kitty were both silent until they were back in the SUV.

"I guess that was a no," Priscilla said as she started the engine. Kitty handed her the note.

Dear Kitty,

I hope you'll forgive me calling you that, but since we did write back and forth several times and since your aunt Katherine was so fond of talking about you and your mother, I feel as if we are old friends. Please forgive me too, for the deception and then for being too cowardly to admit what I had done. It's not right that you should find out about your aunt's death the way you did or that I should have let you worry about her for so many months, but better a late apology than never one at all. It is kind of you to want to keep writing to me, but I think it best that you do not. Please remember your aunt Katherine fondly. The two of us were great friends, and I miss her every day.

Caroline Waterman

Priscilla handed the note back to Kitty. "I'm sorry. She sounds so sad."

"I know. I'm not mad at her, and I understand why she kept writing me. I don't know her at all, of course, but if she's so lonely she'd pretend to be someone else just to have someone to write to, I don't know why she wouldn't want to keep doing it under her own name. I wouldn't mind."

"Well, maybe she'll change her mind someday." Priscilla put the SUV in gear and drove away. "At least you made the offer."

Kitty sighed and didn't reply.

Priscilla smiled at her. "I think we need to go get that birthday present now. I promise you'll be smiling by the time we find exactly the right one."

"Oh no, you aren't!" Kitty looked at Priscilla with the biggest grin on her face when they turned off County Road and pulled up in front of the animal shelter. "You're getting your cousin a pet for her birthday?"

Priscilla nodded eagerly. "She lost her dog over a year ago, and I know she still misses him. I think it's time she had another one."

"You don't think you ought to check with her first? I mean, she's the one who'll be taking care of it and everything."

"I know. I also know she really wants another dog, but she keeps talking herself out of it. If somebody doesn't give her a little shove, she'll never get one, and that would be a shame. She's a widow, and I think she'd be happier if she wasn't alone in the house."

Kitty looked at the well-kept fenced yard where several puppies were playing. "This looks like a good place."

"It's no kill and cage free. And the people here are great. They really care about the animals."

A volunteer showed them all the puppies. There were so many cute ones that Priscilla was afraid she'd have a hard time choosing, but she knew the right one the moment she saw it. It took only a few minutes for her to fill out all the paperwork and pay the adoption fee. The shelter agreed to keep the puppy for her until the next day. She would pick it up before she and her cousins got together for lunch.

Kitty laughed when they got back into the SUV. "You know, I'd forgotten how much fun we used to have back in Kansas. Thanks for letting me stay a while."

"We did have fun. I'm sorry things didn't turn out any happier about your aunt, but I'm glad we found each other again. I think you'll love the island, and I'm sure my cousins will love meeting you."

As they drove, Priscilla told her more about Gail, Trudy, and Joan, and before long, they were pulling up at the pet supply store.

"You don't mind, do you? I can't very well surprise Joan with a dog and then not give her at least the basic necessities."

"No problem. Maybe I'll pick up something to take back to Emily."

"Emily?"

Kitty smiled and began fishing in her purse, eventually pulling out a picture of a white-and-tabby-spotted cat with sea-green eyes. "That's Em. She just showed up on our back porch one morning when Keith and I were out there drinking coffee, and then she came inside with us as if she owned the place. She didn't have a microchip, though she does now, and we checked around to see if anyone was missing her, but nobody ever claimed her. So now she's ours. Well, mostly she's Keith's, if he's home. I'll do if there's nobody else."

"I think our pets adopt us," Priscilla said as they went inside. "I'm always amazed how perfect they end up being once we get them home. I wasn't expecting Jake at all when I found him, but now I don't know what I'd do without him."

It didn't take long for them to find the supplies Joan would need for her new puppy: a collar and leash, the food the shelter had recommended, a training crate, a few toys. Kitty found a package of catnip mice for Emily, and they got in line to check out.

"Priscilla!"

Priscilla turned to see Gerald O'Bannon hurrying up to her.

"Gerald. Hi. I didn't expect to see you here."

There was a smile in his hazel eyes, and he looked dashing as always in his Coast Guard uniform. "I'm stocking up for Sammy." He shifted the bag of dogfood on his shoulder. "She's not a hesitant eater."

Priscilla laughed and then pulled Kitty up next to her. "Kitty, this is Gerald. I used to know Kitty and her husband back in Kansas. We bumped into each other yesterday."

Gerald removed his cap, and a lock of wavy hair fell over his forehead. "Good to meet you, Kitty."

"How's that grandbaby?" Priscilla asked with a smile. Gerald's daughter Aggie had given birth to a sweet little girl not long ago.

Gerald beamed at her. "She's an angel. I'd show you some pictures, but it's hard to stop once I start, and your friend would be bored stiff." He smiled at Kitty. "Are you getting a dog?"

Kitty glanced at Priscilla. "Not me."

"A friend for Jake?" Gerald asked, lifting one eyebrow.

"Don't tell anyone," Priscilla said, lowering her voice as she leaned closer. "It's a present for Joan's birthday."

"Ah." Gerald gave her a nod and then turned to Kitty. "Do you live here now?"

Kitty shook her head. "Just visiting. Actually, I came to look up an aunt of mine."

"Well, that's good. I hope you had a nice visit with your aunt."

Kitty sighed. "I found out she passed away a little while ago."

"Oh." Gerald turned his cap in his hand, looking to Priscilla to bail him out. "I'm sorry."

"Her aunt used to work for Miss Waterman," Priscilla explained. "She passed away a couple of years ago."

"Waterman, eh?" Gerald gave a low whistle. "She's sure got folks in an uproar right now."

Kitty's eyes darted from him to Priscilla. "What do you mean?"

"It's a local thing, I guess," Priscilla said. "She owns a museum about the Cavanaughs she's going to close and a lot of undeveloped land she's planning to sell to developers."

"It's not only home builders," Gerald said, moving up in the line with them. "Some guy wants to put up a bunch of high-density apartment complexes. It would double or triple the population in Tisbury."

Priscilla caught a startled breath. "But that would ruin everything. W-we wouldn't recognize the place after that."

"Tell me about it," Gerald said. "So much for historic Vineyard Haven."

"Isn't there anything you can do?" Kitty asked. "Surely there's a town council or something that can stop that kind of thing. Believe me, I've dealt with my share of roadblocks in some of the sales I've worked on."

"I don't think it's a done deal yet," Gerald told her. "And you can bet there's plenty of discussion going on. I guess we just have to wait and see what happens." He shook his head. "I'd hate for us to lose that beautiful view."

No one said anything until the cashier cleared her throat.

"Next in line, please."

"Oops," Priscilla said, "that's us." She moved up and started unloading her cart.

"Oh, man," Gerald said when he saw the collar. "I forgot to get a new one for Sammy. Hers is about worn out. It was good to meet you, Kitty. I'll see you later, Priscilla."

"Remember what I said," Priscilla told him as she put the leash on the counter. "Don't spoil the surprise."

He gave her a wink. "No one will ever get a word out of me. But if you ask me, it's about time."

He walked off toward the dog section of the store, and Priscilla finished her purchase.

"Well, well," Kitty said when they were driving back to the cottage. She looked slyly pleased. "Is that what I think it is?"

"If you think it's a friend of mine, you're absolutely right."

"Do all your friends make you turn pink like that?"

"Don't be silly," Priscilla said, but she could feel the warmth in her cheeks intensify. "Okay, he's a nice-looking guy. And he's a nice guy. But, really, we're only friends."

"All right," Kitty said, "but there's nothing wrong with having a handsome sailor looking after you."

"I guess there are worse things," Priscilla admitted. "Now, what would you like to do? A little sightseeing?"

"That would be great. Actually, that museum you were talking about interests me. Aunt Katherine worked for the Cavanaugh family before she worked for Miss Waterman. Maybe there's something in that museum about her. She was the maid or housekeeper or something for Rosie Cavanaugh in the sixties. I'm sure there wouldn't be anything about her specifically, but she might be in the background of a picture or something. It would be fun to look." Her expression turned wistful. "I don't know for sure if I'd be able to pick her out, but I might. I don't remember much about how she looked besides the pictures my mother had of her. I guess she wouldn't have aged that much during the time she worked for Rosie."

"I think that sounds like a lovely idea. Shall we have a look at the museum tomorrow before it's gone?"

Kitty's eyes sparkled. "That would be great."

CHAPTER FOUR

Priscilla's cottage wasn't far from the museum, and it took only a few minutes to drive there on Friday morning.

"Looks like we won't be the only ones visiting," Priscilla said, seeing the black, late-model Lamborghini parked out front.

"Only the poorest ones," Kitty said, eyeing the sleek car.

Priscilla grinned and then looked more closely at the car. Particularly the license plate. CAV 4. He'd certainly be rich enough to have a car like this.

"What are you puzzling over?" Kitty asked.

"Maybe nothing," Priscilla said. "But I'll tell you if I'm right."

With Kitty at her heels, Priscilla went up to the door. She was about to turn the knob when she heard something and stopped to listen. There was, if not a full-blown argument, a very passionate discussion going on inside the museum.

"I told you I don't want to sell."

Priscilla was almost certain that was Malcolm Waterman's voice. There was a certain nasal quality to it that was very distinctive. The voice that answered him was rich and deep, a voice that wouldn't be out of place doing broadcasting or high-quality voice-overs.

"Half of this stuff is ours already."

"I know. I'll give back what you loaned us if you insist. The rest isn't for sale. Not even to you."

Kitty looked anxiously at Priscilla. Feeling awkward about eavesdropping, Priscilla knocked and then opened the door. Malcolm stood beside the display case that held all the Cavanaugh medals, looking flustered. The man with him was tall and handsome in an all-American sort of way. Not young anymore, of course, but still not yet fifty, tan and fit. She hadn't been wrong, then, about the car.

"Hello," she said, hovering in the doorway. "All right if we come in?"

Malcolm didn't look as if it were the least bit all right, but he nodded. "We're open all day. Are you looking for something in particular this time?"

"My friend is in town," Priscilla said, "and she wanted to see the museum while she's here."

Kitty gave both men a tentative smile. "My aunt used to work for the Cavanaughs when she was young." She tilted her head to one side. "Aren't you—aren't you Mr. Cavanaugh?"

He thrust out his hand, suddenly all smiles and campaign promises. "I certainly am, but you just call me Rowan. Everybody does." He shook Kitty's hand and then Priscilla's. "And what was your aunt's name, ma'am?"

"Katherine Evans," Kitty told him. "I think she worked for your grandmother. Rosie."

Rowan Cavanaugh nodded slowly. "Yes, she did. She was Grandmother's personal maid. I don't remember her, of course.

That was before my time, but I remember my father talking about her from when he was a boy. I believe she left shortly after Grandmother died. Must have been, oh, sometime in the late sixties."

"I think so," Kitty said. "She absolutely adored your grandmother."

Cavanaugh flashed a wide smile at her. "Everyone did. And from what Dad said, she was very fond of your aunt. I, uh..." He glanced briefly at Malcolm. "To tell the truth, I'm trying to track down a few things of my grandmother's, and I'm wondering if your aunt might have had anything of hers. Keepsakes perhaps?"

"I wouldn't know," Kitty said. "She never told me about it if she did."

"Ah, well, I just thought I'd ask. Of course, if Malcolm here would be reasonable about selling me the rest of these things, I might feel as if I had most of my family's keepsakes back in the family."

Priscilla looked at Malcolm, puzzled. "I thought your aunt wanted to sell."

"She's selling this house and property. The museum collection, the things that aren't on loan, belonged to her and to my father. I inherited his portion after he died. I'm not interested in selling."

Priscilla nodded and studied the display again. One of the ribbons was tilted slightly forward against its velvet backdrop, and she leaned a little closer, frowning. She smiled abruptly when she noticed Malcolm looking at her, and then drifted to an exhibit about Rosie Cavanaugh's war work.

"I told you I'd make it worth your while," Cavanaugh said, oblivious to their exchange.

Malcolm's mouth tightened primly. "And I told you I wasn't interested."

There was a flash of fury in Cavanaugh's eyes, but then he managed a tight smile. "I guess that's that, then." He turned again to Kitty. "You didn't happen to go through your aunt's things when she passed away?"

Kitty shook her head. "I didn't even know she had died until yesterday."

Cavanaugh's burly eyebrows went up. "I see. Who would have seen to her estate, do you know?"

Kitty laughed softly. "I don't know that you could call it an estate. She was a live-in housekeeper. I don't think she had more than clothes and that sort of thing. Maybe a little costume jewelry. Nothing that would have been of value to anyone. That is, if she'd had anyone to leave anything to."

As they talked, Priscilla moved back to the display of campaign ribbons, but then, seeing Malcolm watching her again, she moved back to Kitty's side.

"It would be very helpful if I could speak to whoever was with her when she died," Cavanaugh said. "Do you know where that was?"

"Oh, yes," Kitty told him. "She was working for Miss Caroline Waterman. I guess you wouldn't have known that. She kept house and looked after Miss Waterman. I suppose it would have been a lot like what she did for your grandmother Rosie: light cleaning, planning menus, cooking, looking after her appointments and correspondence. That's what my mother told me."

"Help like that is hard to come by." Cavanaugh nodded sympathetically. "I'm sure Miss Caroline was sorry to lose her." He eyed Malcolm once again. "So you must have known Katherine Evans as well."

"Not really." Malcolm shrugged his thin shoulders. "She took care of things at the house, but it wasn't as if I had any reason to spend time with her, and it's been quite a while since I was at Aunt Caroline's."

"That's too bad." Cavanaugh smiled again at Kitty. "You might have told us all something more about this lady's aunt. It might have been a great comfort."

Priscilla glanced at Kitty, not liking how either man was looking at them. "I guess we ought to be going."

Kitty looked puzzled, but she didn't protest.

"We've got some errands to run and then a lunch to go to," Priscilla told the two men as she took her friend's arm. "We'll come back, Mr. Waterman, when you're not so busy. Come on, Kitty. We're going to be late."

"What was that about?" Kitty asked once they had shut the museum door behind them and were headed down the walk.

"I don't know. Come on."

They were halfway to the animal shelter before Priscilla said anything else. "I didn't like how Rowan Cananaugh was acting."

Kitty shrugged. "I thought he was very nice. I mean, for a famous person and everything."

"He was certainly putting a lot of pressure on Malcolm, don't you think?"

"Maybe." Kitty frowned. "I'm sure Aunt Katherine didn't have anything he'd want. I don't even have anything of hers except a few Christmas and birthday cards. Certainly not anything that belonged to Rosie Cavanaugh."

"At least he knows that now. He can talk to Miss Waterman about anything your aunt might have had at her house when she died."

"Good luck with that," Kitty said, and her frown deepened. "It's funny that Aunt Katherine worked for Rosie Cavanaugh and then for Miss Waterman, isn't it?"

"I don't know. If the Watermans and the Cavanaughs were close, it seems reasonable to me that if Rosie's death put your aunt out of a job and Miss Waterman needed a housekeeper-companion, it would be a very natural move."

"I suppose." Kitty sighed and looked out the window at the soggy scenery passing by. "I still think it's strange that Miss Waterman would have kept writing to me all this time after Aunt Katherine died."

"I guess it is." Priscilla turned onto June Avenue. "And if she was lonely enough to do that, why doesn't she want to keep writing now? Maybe she's embarrassed about your finding out. She said she meant to tell you last fall and never quite knew how to do it. That could be all there is to it." By then they were at the animal shelter, and she pulled up at the curb. "Whatever her reasons are, there's not much we can do about it. Why don't we let it go for the time being and concentrate on having a good time today, okay?"

Kitty exhaled heavily, and the worry in her expression faded. "That sounds good to me."

Joan's cottage looked picturesque even when the garden wasn't yet in full bloom. The yard was beautifully laid out and carefully tended. It could almost have been mistaken for something along the English coastline.

"You should see it in July," Priscilla said as she got out of her SUV.

Kitty got out too. "It's lovely exactly as it is. So Joan is the nature lover, right?"

"Right. She also works in the mornings as an ultrasound technician."

Kitty frowned. "I thought she was a dental hygienist."

"No, that's Gail."

"The widow," Kitty said, nodding.

"No, that's Joan. Gail's divorced."

"But the other one's married." Kitty looked at her hopefully. "Right?"

"Right. That's Trudy."

Kitty sighed.

"Don't worry," Priscilla said with a chuckle as she lifted the pet carrier out of the back of the SUV. "You'll get it all straight. And I'll help you."

"You're *sure* they won't mind me coming too?"

Priscilla gave her a playful scowl. "If you ask me that again, you'll have to eat in the car."

Kitty laughed and followed Priscilla to the door. Before Priscilla could ring the doorbell, the door opened and Trudy hurried out, blue eyes sparkling and platinum-blonde curls bouncing.

"Hi! I was watching for you!" Trudy tried to peek into the crate. "Is this what I think it is? Oh my goodness! Joan will be so surprised!" She smiled at Kitty. "You must be Kitty. We're so glad to have you! Come in!"

"Kitty," Priscilla said, "this is my cousin Trudy Galvin. Is Dan here, Trudy?"

Trudy shook her head. "Of course not! My husband would rather be shot than be stuck at a hen party."

They went inside and found Joan and Gail sitting on the couch, talking. Joan looked at the pet carrier suspiciously, but Priscilla set it down behind the couch, hidden from Joan's view.

"Happy Birthday, Joan!" Priscilla gave her cousin a hug. "This is Kitty Merrick from Wheatfield. Kitty, this is Joan Abernathy, the birthday girl, and my other cousin, Gail Smith."

Kitty gave them both a shy smile. "Hello."

"All right," Joan said, narrowing her dark eyes. "Now that we all know each other, I want to know exactly what is in that carrier."

Priscilla grinned. "It's your birthday present. Sit down and I'll give it to you."

"Priscilla..."

"Go on. Sit down."

Joan sat, and Gail and Trudy grinned at each other.

"Now close your eyes," Priscilla ordered, and with a sigh, Joan obeyed.

"No peeking," Gail warned, a twinkle in her gray-blue eyes as Priscilla took the puppy out of the crate and set her in Joan's lap. The dog gave a little whimper, the first sound Priscilla had heard out of her, and Joan's eyes flew open.

"Oh. Oh!"

The little dog sat looking up at her, eyebrows quivering, uncertain and eager all at once, whimpering softly again. After a long moment, Joan finally wrapped the squirming tan-and-white bundle in her arms, getting a profusion of nuzzling licks in return.

"Look at you." Joan held the puppy up so she could see her better. "What a precious little thing you are."

"Her name is Sister," Priscilla told her cousin. "The shelter says she's three months old and that she's a blue heeler mix."

"She doesn't look like any blue heeler I ever saw," Gail said in a stage whisper.

"Aww, I don't care." Joan cuddled her close again. "I think Sister is absolutely perfect."

"Good." Priscilla beamed at her. "I'm so glad you like her. I knew she was the right one the minute I saw her."

"But I don't—" Joan looked longingly into Sister's hopeful black eyes and then shook her head. "I'm not really ready for this. I don't have food or anything for her. I'm not—"

"I got you everything you need," Priscilla assured her. "Everything's in the SUV. I got a big bag of the food the shelter was feeding her, so you know she'll like it. I got a leash. She's got her collar on already. I have a crate for her right here. What else do you need?"

Joan glanced at Gail, only a hint of panic in her expression. "Nothing, I guess. It's just...I don't know if I'm ready."

"You've been saying that for months," Trudy said.

"And you've looked longingly at every puppy you've seen that whole time," Gail added.

"I know nothing can ever replace Champ," Priscilla said gently. "But look at that little face. Do you really want to tell her she has to go back to the shelter?"

Joan looked down at Sister. Sister looked back, and then she tilted her head to one side, her little forehead wrinkled. It was a perfect "don't you love me?" pose. Joan didn't stand a chance.

"Poor little baby." She cuddled Sister close again. "All right," she said to Priscilla, smiling at last. "And thank you. She had to be the cutest one in that shelter."

"No contest," Priscilla assured her. "And happy birthday."

"Yes, happy birthday," Kitty said. "And thanks for letting me come to your party."

"I'm glad you could come," Joan said. "What do you all think? Shall we have lunch while it's hot?"

"Good idea!" Trudy said.

Everyone stood up. Joan kissed Sister on the top of her fuzzy head and then put her back in the carrier. "Only until we finish eating, sweetie, and then we'll let you out again." She looked at Priscilla. "She is house-trained, isn't she?"

"Uh, I think so. That shelter doesn't use cages, so I assume she must be."

Joan shook her head. "I guess we'll find out."

CHAPTER FIVE

To celebrate Joan's birthday, Trudy and Gail had fixed a scrumptious meal of leek-and-cauliflower soup, broiled striped bass, roasted corn, and tomato salad.

"If you come back in the summer," Joan told Kitty, "you could have pan-seared scup."

"Scup?" Kitty asked uncertainly, and Joan smiled.

"It's only fish fillets. Some people call it porgy, but we call it scup."

"Maybe I can try it sometime," Kitty told her, "but this bass is delicious. It's nice to have fresh seafood all the time, isn't it? Keith and I have really enjoyed it since we moved to Portland."

"Fresh-caught is hard to get in Kansas," Priscilla said with a grin.

"So what have the two of you been doing today?" Joan asked. She glanced toward the dog carrier. "Besides getting my present."

"We stopped by the Cavanaugh Museum," Priscilla said, thinking back on the visit. "Kitty's aunt used to work for them, and she wanted to see it."

"Mr. Cavanaugh was actually there." Kitty's eyes lit with excitement. "You know, I've seen him on TV a million times, like everybody else. I don't support him politically myself, but he is sort of famous, isn't he? It's almost like meeting American royalty."

"Didn't you like him?" Trudy asked Priscilla. "You look like you didn't have a very good time."

Priscilla shrugged and ate another spoonful of the delicious soup. "It was a little more interesting than I was expecting. When we got there, he and Malcolm Waterman were squabbling over Malcolm selling him some of the museum's items."

"He didn't want to? I thought the museum was closing."

"Evidently Malcolm doesn't care. He doesn't want to sell. I don't know what his aunt is going to say about that, since she does want to sell. Apparently they have some kind of joint ownership." Priscilla frowned. "And there was something else I noticed. Something might be wrong. Maybe. I need to do some research."

"What is it?" Trudy asked, her blue eyes wide. "Another Cavanaugh scandal?"

"I don't know about that," Priscilla said.

"It was something in that display case, wasn't it?" Kitty said. "I thought you were looking at it strangely. I don't think Malcolm liked how you were studying it either."

"It's hardly anything. I'm not even sure I should be alarmed. But..."

"But what?" Trudy urged. "What?"

"Well, it was one of those campaign ribbons," Priscilla began. "The clasp on one of them didn't look right."

"Campaign ribbons?" Gail asked.

"You know." Priscilla held up the thumb and forefinger of each hand, making a long rectangle, and rested them where a shirt pocket would be. "Those little pins with different colored bars on them that military men wear. They show where each man served and what kind of honors he earned."

"Oh, that kind of ribbon." Trudy giggled. "I was thinking more on the lines of a big ribbon like you get when you win a prize at the state fair."

Joan chuckled.

"Anyway, a few years ago, Gary and I were trying to find a replacement for one that a man in our church received when he was in World War II. We found a copy, but he said it wasn't authentic. He said the one he got in the war had what looked like a big safety pin for a clasp. The new one had two short pins sticking straight out of the back and then those little butterfly clutches, almost like earring backs, to hold them on once the pins were poked through the uniform. He told us that only the top brass had pins like that, and that his lighter-weight uniform would have torn with that sort of thing. The ribbon in the display case had a clasp like that even though the placard said it was awarded to a Sergeant Cavanaugh, which makes me wonder about its authenticity."

"Well, that's odd," Gail said, helping herself to more corn.

Priscilla shrugged. "Maybe the man from my church was mistaken. Or maybe there were some of each, and he just wasn't aware of it. Still, Malcolm sure didn't like me looking at that ribbon."

"You think the one in the case was a fake?" Kitty asked. "Even the real thing couldn't be worth that much, could it?"

"If it was part of a large collection, it could be, especially to a real history buff."

"Wow."

"I'd like to find out more," Priscilla said. "Malcolm might not like me coming back and snooping around again, though."

Trudy clutched Joan's arm. "We could go! We could go look around and report back."

"Trudy," Gail began.

"No, better than that, all three of us could go! And two of you could talk to Malcolm and distract him while I see what other fakes he has in there. Then Priscilla won't have to go back and be conspicuous."

"Like you wouldn't be conspicuous," Gail muttered.

Joan lowered her fork. "And exactly how are you going to know what is authentic and what's not?"

Trudy frowned at her, but before she could reply, Priscilla held up both hands.

"I think we all just need to wait and see what I can find out about those campaign ribbons, all right? Maybe this isn't anything at all. I'll do some research and let you know what I find out."

Kitty's forehead wrinkled. "I guess it's not good to have fakes in a museum, but if they're his own fakes, there's nothing illegal about that, is there?"

"Except," Priscilla reminded her, "they're only partially owned by him. His aunt might not be too happy to find out some of the objects on display aren't authentic."

Nobody seemed to know what to say to that, and they ate for a few minutes in silence.

Finally Joan stood up. "I think I'd better check on my birthday present."

Priscilla watched as Joan went into the living room where Sister was sitting in her carrier, looking forlorn. Seeing Joan, the puppy gave a little yip and leaped to her feet, wagging her tail furiously and sticking as much of her nose as possible through the bars.

"You're all right, honey," Joan told her, petting her nose. "We'll be through in a little bit, and then you can come out."

As soon as Joan turned back toward the table, the puppy started to whine. It wasn't a very loud whine, but it was certainly pitiful.

Joan turned back. "You're okay. You're all right."

Sister was still whining when Joan and Priscilla sat down again.

"She'll get used to it," Gail assured her.

"I'm sure she will," Priscilla said. "The shelter she was in didn't have cages, so maybe she isn't familiar with carriers either. She just needs time."

Joan looked over at the carrier again, biting her lip, and Priscilla patted her arm.

"I'm sorry I didn't think to buy her any toys while I was at the store."

"I suppose she would like something to play with," Joan said, and then, looking as if she had made a decision, she got up again. "Excuse me, everyone. I'll be right back."

She disappeared into the bedroom and returned a moment later with a short, thick piece of rope that had been tied in a knot. It looked well chewed.

"How about this, sweetie? I don't think Champ would have minded sharing."

Joan opened the carrier door, gave the rope to Sister, and then closed the door again. The puppy tried to push her way out, but she was too late, and she started her soft whine again. Again Joan stroked the quivering little nose and then went resolutely back to her lunch.

"Sorry about that," she said as she sat again, and she looked relieved when the whining stopped entirely. "Kitty, you said your aunt worked for the Cavanaughs. Is she the reason you came to the island?"

"She is, actually, though I came a little too late."

By the time Kitty and Priscilla had told the cousins everything they had found out about Katherine Evans's death, Gail had served Joan's special birthday dessert, honey-roasted pears.

"So she worked for the Cavanaughs and for the Watermans," Gail said.

Kitty nodded. "That must have been awfully interesting, especially everything that happened after the Second World War. That was when the Cavanaughs really got famous."

Joan pushed away her plate. "Oh, I'm stuffed. But everything was delicious. Those pears were heavenly. Thank you, Gail. Thank you, Trudy. This was a wonderful lunch."

"You're welcome," Gail said.

"Happy birthday," Trudy added.

"Thanks for letting me barge in," Kitty said. "I've enjoyed meeting all of you. And Sister."

Joan looked toward the crate. Sister was staring back at her, the knotted rope in her mouth. "Maybe we'd better let her join us now."

Sister greeted Joan with ecstatic full-body wagging and licks all over her face. Laughing, Joan sat down on the couch with her.

"Why don't all of you come in here now?" Joan called. "We'll tidy up the dishes in a little while."

They gathered in the living room again, and Gail sat next to Kitty. "I'm sorry you didn't get to see your aunt. Was she your father's sister or your mother's?"

"Neither." Kitty smiled. "She was actually married to my mother's brother, but he died in a plane crash on the day I was born."

Trudy shook her head. "That's so sad."

Kitty nodded. "It could have been worse. He had borrowed a friend's plane, a little private one, and he asked my father to go up with him. But knowing I was about to be born, my father said he'd better not."

"Your poor mother," Priscilla said.

"And poor Aunt Katherine. Anyway, she moved out here when I wasn't very old, but I'll always remember how nice she was. She always treated me like I was special. She was that way in her letters too."

"It's a good way to be remembered," Joan said, cuddling Sister closer, and the puppy nuzzled her neck.

"I guess that's what bothers me still about those letters Miss Waterman sent me. They were so like what Aunt Katherine would have written, I would never have believed they were from anyone else."

Priscilla reached over to pet the puppy that was now half-asleep against Joan's shoulder, thinking for a moment. "I suppose, if your aunt always shared your cards and letters with Miss Waterman, she probably shared her letters to you too. Miss Waterman would have known the kinds of things your aunt wrote to you and her style of writing and everything else."

"The funny part is her not wanting to meet you in person," Trudy said. "It would be a lot easier if she'd just talk to you."

"I wonder if she'll talk to Mr. Cavanaugh," Kitty said, and Trudy looked at her, eyes wide.

"Do you think he'll really go see her?"

Kitty shrugged. "Their families used to be close, and he sure seemed eager to find anything and everything that once belonged to his grandmother. He was asking me about anything I knew about, and there was nothing I could tell him. I do think that, if his grandmother did give something to my aunt, it would very likely still be at the Waterman house."

Joan chuckled. "Good luck to anyone trying to get in there, even Rowan Neville Cavanaugh the Fourth."

The five of them chatted for a while longer, and then they all tidied up from lunch and made sure Joan's kitchen was sparkling clean. They left Joan to take Sister for a walk around her new neighborhood.

"I like your cousins," Kitty said as they drove back to Priscilla's cottage.

Priscilla smiled. "So do I. They've made me feel so at home here. I'm sorry I didn't get to know them before now."

"At least your daughter doesn't have to worry about your being here without anyone."

"Yes, please tell her that."

That made Kitty laugh a little, and then she drew a deep breath. "I guess I ought to call the airlines and see when I can get a flight. I just—I hate to leave without knowing anything else. What if Aunt Katherine did leave some personal things behind? I'd love to see them. I wouldn't feel as if she'd somehow disappeared without a trace. And maybe some of it would be about my mother. She died ten years ago, and I feel like there was so much I should have done while she was still here."

Priscilla didn't say anything for a moment. She couldn't help thinking about her own parents. Even though her relationship with them had been close and loving, there were still things she wished she'd done—and hadn't done—while they were still alive. "I guess that's pretty common," she said finally. "It's human nature to have a few regrets, to feel as if we could have done better once it's too late to do anything at all."

They drove on a little farther and finally stopped at an intersection.

"Well, should we try again?" Priscilla looked at the turn to their right. "That's the way back to Miss Waterman's."

"Do you think we should? I mean, it's not like we'd be asking to see Miss Waterman again."

"Right. What do you think?"

There was a gleam in Kitty's dark eyes. "Let's do it."

The dog barking furiously behind her, Anna Vaden opened the door and looked at Priscilla and Kitty, stone-faced. "I thought the last time was actually going to be the last time."

Kitty ducked her head a little, as if she were a naughty child at school.

"We thought of one more thing," Priscilla said, very serenely. "We were wondering if Katherine might have left behind any personal items. I realize there's not likely to be anything of value, but if she kept any family mementos, letters or photographs or anything like that, her niece would really love to have them."

"I wouldn't know about that," Anna said, tight-lipped. "That was before my time."

"But Miss Waterman—"

"My guess is she would have thrown out anything of that sort two years ago or more."

"That doesn't really seem like her, does it?" Priscilla asked the housekeeper. "If Katherine worked for her all those years and she didn't see anyone else, surely Miss Waterman would have kept something of hers as a remembrance. Maybe in the attic or something?"

Anna scowled. "Do you want me to ask?"

"That would be very kind of you," Priscilla said, her tone very sweet.

With a sniff, the housekeeper shut the door. She was back a moment later.

"Miss Waterman says she thinks there may be a few items in a dresser upstairs. She wants to look through it to see. If there's anything to do with your aunt, she'll send it along to you tomorrow." Anna produced a pencil and paper. "If you'll write down your phone number and address, I'll see she gets it."

Priscilla did as she asked, adding her name and Kitty's, and a thank-you, and then gave the pencil and paper back.

"We'll be in contact," Anna said, and she shut the door.

"Well, that's something anyway," Kitty said as they drove back to the cottage. "But I guess that means I'll be on your hands for a day or two more. I hope that's okay."

"Sure. I'll be glad for the company. In fact, if you'd like, you can help me with the museum I'm working on for the lighthouse."

"I'd love to. The history here is so interesting. We're definitely not in Kansas anymore."

Jake was waiting to go outside when they got home, so Priscilla took him and Kitty for a short walk along the beach. Jake was certainly ready for a little exercise.

Kitty laughed at the way he trotted along, interested in everything they passed as if he'd never seen it before that very moment.

"I think he's the perfect dog for you," she puffed, doing her best to stretch her short legs. "You both walk fast!"

Priscilla slowed a little. "Sorry about that. Yeah, Jake and I cover a lot of ground every day." She told Kitty about finding the red-and-white stray after he was hit by a car. "We met literally by accident, but I think we were meant to be together."

"Oh, absolutely," Kitty said. "He's darling. I think your cousin liked her birthday present too."

"I hope so. Normally I think it's a bad idea to surprise some-one with a pet, but Joan needed somebody to give her a little nudge."

"I could tell she was taken with Sister too. I don't know how anybody could resist that precious little face."

"We'll check on them tomorrow if we have a chance, okay?" Priscilla said as they walked down to the end of the dock.

"That would be great. You know, I'd love to treat you both to lunch tomorrow. Do you think Joan would be available?"

"We can give her a call to make sure, but if I were guessing, I'd say yes. She usually works at the clinic from nine to noon, so that ought to work out great for lunch."

Priscilla called her cousin once she and Kitty and Jake got back to the cottage, and Joan said she would love to go out to lunch with them the next day. Priscilla had just hung up the phone when it rang again. This time it was Anna Vaden.

CHAPTER SIX

M iss Waterman did find some things your friend might want to have," the housekeeper told Priscilla, not sounding any friendlier than she had earlier that day. "Is there a convenient time I could bring them by tomorrow?"

"I can't wait to see what Miss Waterman found," Priscilla replied, giving Kitty an excited smile. "I hate to trouble you to come here, though. Kitty and I will be out at lunchtime tomorrow. Would it be convenient for us to come by and pick up the items then? Then we won't need to trouble you again."

"Humph." The housekeeper's disdain was palpable even over the telephone. "I suppose that would be all right. We'll be home."

"Thank—" Priscilla laughed softly at the abrupt click. "I guess that's the end of the conversation. Thank you, anyway."

"What did she find?" Kitty asked, her eyes bright. "What did she say?"

"Not much, but we can pick up whatever it is tomorrow at lunchtime. Now, what do you think? Would you like to help me set up a display about Llewellyn Latham, the first owner of the Misty Harbor Lighthouse?"

They spent a pleasant afternoon setting out the display. Kitty's experience in selling houses had given her a good eye for design, and she gave Priscilla a lot of practical hints for making attractive exhibits. She asked a lot of questions too, which made Priscilla rethink a few of her ideas for other displays in the museum. When they were both tired enough to quit, they went back to the cottage, had a simple dinner, and then chatted as they baked oatmeal cookies. They were both eager to see what Miss Waterman had that had once belonged to Katherine Evans. Priscilla could only hope that Kitty wouldn't be disappointed by whatever it was.

"Kitty's as good as a test audience," Priscilla told Joan while the three of them were at the rustic Red Cat Kitchen for lunch the next day. "Sometimes what makes perfect sense to me doesn't to other people."

"I didn't do much," Kitty protested, toying with the spoon in her lobster bisque. "What you have is very interesting, though, and I wanted to know more."

"You were a big help with everything," Priscilla assured her. "Too bad you can't stay until I have everything done."

Kitty laughed. "I don't know if my husband or my boss *or* my client would appreciate that."

"Thanks for coming over yesterday," Joan said. "It was good to have you."

"I enjoyed it. How's Sister doing?"

Joan sighed. "Well, other than whining most of the night and having an accident on my kitchen floor and eating one of my shoes, she's fine."

Priscilla cringed. "Oh, Joan, I'm sorry. Maybe I shouldn't have given her to you."

"She's all right," Joan said, though her smile wasn't entirely convincing. "She'll learn. And that accident was my fault. I got distracted and waited too long to take her out. I guess it's been a while since I've had to think about anybody but myself. And even longer since I had a puppy. At my age, getting up every couple of hours all night takes some getting used to."

"I'm sorry," Priscilla said again. "I hope you two are getting along otherwise."

Now Joan's smile turned warm. "She's awfully sweet. She follows me everywhere when she's not in her crate, and she loves to sleep in my lap."

"The lady at the shelter told me she didn't like to be alone. I guess she was serious."

"I think that's darling," Kitty said. "There's nothing like snuggling with a puppy or a kitten."

"How long do you think you'll be staying?" Joan asked Kitty, taking a bite of her soup.

"Not much longer. I'll have to get back to work, and I guess there's not much more for me to find out here. I am curious about what Aunt Katherine left behind, but it probably won't be much of anything. I mean, I'll be happy to have something to remember her by, especially if it's something to do with my mother, but that's about it."

Priscilla stirred some cream into her coffee and took a sip. "Mr. Cavanaugh was certainly interested in what she might have left behind. And in whatever was at the museum."

"I guess you heard about it too." The waitress, a petite redhead who seemed hardly old enough to hold a job, came to the table with a heavily laden tray and looked eager to repeat what she'd heard. "The break-in."

Priscilla could only gape at her. "There was a break-in at the Cavanaugh Museum?"

"Where'd you hear that?" Joan asked.

"One of my regulars told me about it a little while ago. She lives not far from there and had to pass it on the way in. She said there were police all over the place, so she called one of her neighbors who's friends with Malcolm Waterman. The neighbor told her all about it."

"What was taken?" Priscilla asked.

"She didn't know anything really specific about that, only that Mr. Waterman was furious." The waitress set Priscilla's seared salmon in front of her. "I don't blame him. It's not like you can buy all that history stuff at the gas station." She served a crab soufflé to Kitty and stuffed flounder to Joan. "Anything else I can get for you?"

Priscilla shook her head. "You don't know anything else about the break-in, do you?"

"I'm sorry, no. But I have some fresh coffee brewing, and I'll be back in a little while to make sure you all have everything you need."

"What did you say about Mr. Cavanaugh wanting to buy things from the museum?" Joan said once the waitress was gone, her voice low.

"He and Malcolm were having words over it when we were there yesterday," Priscilla said, and she took a bite of her salmon. "Mmm, this is delicious. Anyway, Malcolm wouldn't sell." She looked at Kitty. "Do you think Cavanaugh might have had something to do with the break-in?"

"I don't know. Do you think we should go over there and see what we can find out?"

"Do you want me to come with you?" Joan asked. "Not that I can be of any particular help, but I'd like to know what happened too."

"Why not?" Priscilla ate some of her potatoes au gratin, doing her best not to rush through the meal. "Do you think Sister will be okay?"

"She's in her crate," Joan said. "I don't think another few minutes will make any difference. I'll take her on a good long walk when I get home."

It didn't take them long to finish eating, and then Priscilla drove them over to the museum. She was half-expecting to see yellow police tape over the front door, but there was nothing but a large handwritten Closed sign. Malcolm Waterman was just leaving.

"Closed," he said, glaring at them from behind his thick glasses and waving them off with both hands as they came up the walk. "Nothing to see."

"We heard there was a break-in," Priscilla said. "I'm so sorry. What was taken?"

"What wasn't?" he snapped. "Almost everything is gone now. All of it."

Kitty put one hand over her mouth. "That's terrible. Mr. Cavanaugh will be so upset to know his family's things are gone now."

Malcolm's face twisted into a scowl. "No, he won't. Yesterday afternoon, his people came and took away everything that his family had loaned the museum. Everything that was stolen was mine." He gave them a bitter smile. "Funny how he happened to get his own things out just in the nick of time."

Priscilla glanced at Kitty and then back at Malcolm. "You don't think he—"

"I don't think anything," Malcolm snarled. "I don't have proof against anybody, so I'm not allowed to think. At least that's what the police tell me."

"What did they say?" Priscilla asked. "Did they find anything that would tell them who broke in?"

He shrugged impatiently. "They said someone broke the lock on the back door to get in, and whoever it was got out the same way. It had to have been late last night or very early this morning. I stayed until almost eleven last night, trying to get the things I had left packed up. I arrived this morning before eight, meaning to finish the job. I knew something was wrong the minute I opened the front door. I had left a light on in the entryway like I always do, and it was out. Then I saw that a couple of the display cases were broken. Not really smashed up, as if it were vandalism, but the locks were broken, and everything was gone."

Joan shook her head. "That's awful."

"Tell me about it." Malcolm snorted. "The best part is that I had almost everything already packed up and waiting for them. It couldn't have taken fifteen minutes to grab the rest and haul it all off."

"The police will catch whoever it is, won't they?" Kitty asked, looking hopeful.

Malcolm sneered. "Our little bunch of Keystone Cops?"

Joan glared at him.

"They may not be NY or LAPD," Priscilla said, her mouth tight, "but I wouldn't count them out."

"I'm not holding my breath. I doubt they'll recover my stuff anytime soon." He frowned. "Or anytime at all. Like I said, there's nothing to see here. Please excuse me."

He stalked to the driveway, flung himself into his car, and drove off.

Kitty watched him, her dark eyes troubled. "Priscilla? Do you think we should tell someone what we overheard yesterday? What he and Mr. Cavanaugh were talking about?"

Priscilla looked back at the museum, thinking. Surely someone like Rowan Cavanaugh IV wouldn't be so foolish as to break into someplace to take what he wasn't able to buy. But maybe he would. Some of those powerful political families weren't above such things, though it seemed highly unlikely that, if Cavanaugh was behind the break-in, he would have been personally involved. Families like his always had "people," didn't they?

"I haven't been to the museum in years," Joan said. "To be honest, I don't remember all that much about it, except I loved Rosie Cavanaugh's wedding dress. I hope that wasn't stolen."

"I don't know," Priscilla said. "I'd guess that was one of the items on loan and it still belonged to the Cavanaughs. Maybe they had already taken it before the break-in. I hope so. It's lovely." She narrowed her eyes, thinking. "I wonder, though, how much of that stuff had intrinsic value. Sure it's all interesting to see, but is any of it worth stealing? Especially what Malcolm and his aunt actually own. It's interesting because of who it belonged to, but is it worth actual money?"

"It would be to collectors, I suppose," Joan said. "I couldn't say how much, but if you look at what some rock stars' sweaty 'show worn' T-shirts sell for, you'd be amazed. And who would have stolen that stuff from the museum if it's not worth something?"

"What do you suppose Mr. Cavanaugh was after yesterday?" Kitty asked. "I didn't notice anything in there that was all that important. I mean, sure, it would be important to him since it was all about his family, but it seemed to me that he was interested in something in particular. Maybe I'm imagining it."

Priscilla shook her head. "I got the same impression. I don't know what it could be, though. It was strange, him asking if you had anything."

"It makes me a little nervous now," Kitty said. "I mean, do you think we'll have to testify about what we overheard? I wouldn't want anybody like the Cavanaughs mad at me. I don't know how true the stories are, but you always hear about these influential families having judges and police in their pockets."

Priscilla couldn't deny she'd heard the same sort of thing. "Let's not get too worried about that unless someone brings it up, okay? For now, I guess we'd better go get whatever Miss Waterman has for you."

"I still don't like the sound of that dog," Kitty whispered as they waited for the housekeeper to answer Miss Waterman's door.

"I suppose with just the two of them living here, it's good to have a little protection," Priscilla said. "Though I feel safe with Jake in the house, and he's friendly unless something bad is going on. This dog seems to be ready to bite everybody."

"We are strangers," Joan reminded them. "It could be he—"

"Quiet," someone snarled inside the house. The dog yelped and then was silent. A moment later, the door opened.

"I thought it might be you two," Anna said to Priscilla and Kitty, and then she looked Joan up and down. "I see you brought help with you this time. You didn't need to. I think the two of you could have managed alone."

There was a touch of a smirk on her thin lips as she handed Kitty a large, unlabeled manila envelope.

Kitty looked at it as if she had been expecting more, but then she smiled at the housekeeper. "Thank you very much. Please tell Miss Waterman—"

"She sent you this too." Anna handed her a note. It looked as if it had been written on the same fine notepaper Miss Waterman had used for her earlier message.

Kitty clutched the note tightly. "Please just tell her thank you for me. And tell her I'd love to write to her again if she'd like."

Anna pursed her lips. "I'll tell her again. I'm sure if she changes her mind, she'll let you know."

"How's your dog?" Priscilla asked before the housekeeper could vanish back into the house.

"The dog?" Anna frowned. "He's fine. Why do you ask?"

"He sounded like he was hit or something a minute ago." Priscilla managed to keep her expression coldly serene. "Is he all right?"

"There's nothing wrong with the dog," Anna said, more than a touch of acid in her tone. "Did you want to send the police back out to check on him?"

Before Priscilla could reply, Anna shut the door. There was the distinct sound of a deadbolt being shot into place, and then they heard Anna's voice once more, snapping at the dog to come on. After that there was silence.

"I ought to send the police back out," Priscilla fumed as they drove back to Joan's house. "She has no business treating a dog that way."

"Maybe she thinks she has to," Kitty said. "So he knows she's the boss."

"I don't know about that." Priscilla shook her head. "I don't know enough about guard dogs to know what they do, but it doesn't seem right to me." She was silent for a moment, and then she forced her hands to relax their grip on the steering wheel and looked over at Kitty. "What did Miss Waterman have to say? Anything helpful?"

Kitty unfolded the note and read it over. Then she sighed and folded it again. "Just more of the same. She thanks me for being interested in writing to her, but it's not something she wants to continue. She says for me to remember how much Aunt Katherine loved me and my mother and enjoyed corresponding with us. And she says that, if there's anything else I need to contact her about, she has included the name, address, and phone number of her attorney."

"That sounds pretty final," Joan said from the back seat. "At least you have some of your aunt's things to take home with you. Would you two like to come inside to go through them?" She smiled. "There's a very precious little puppy inside who would love some visitors."

"I'd love to see her again," Priscilla said. "She was definitely the cutest little pup at the shelter."

Joan's smile softened into fondness. "And she sure loves to cuddle."

In a few minutes, they were at Joan's front door, and she was cautioning them to be quiet. "She naps a lot, and I'd be surprised if she wasn't asleep now. I don't know if we'll get past her without her noticing, but we can try."

Priscilla laughed when Joan opened the door and saw Sister standing on the arm of the couch, wagging her little tail and panting happily.

Joan was obviously not amused as she picked up the puppy. "What are you doing? How did you get out?"

"You must not have closed the crate all the way," Priscilla said, and then she bit her lip, seeing at the same time as Joan the sofa pillow stuffing that was now strewn all over the living room floor. "Uh, I'll get your vacuum cleaner."

CHAPTER SEVEN

Priscilla left Joan standing in the living room, holding the puppy, while Kitty quietly picked up bits of stuffing from the couch and coffee table. When she went into the kitchen, Priscilla stopped short. What had once been an unopened loaf of bread was on the kitchen floor, the wrapper chewed open and large bites taken out of the middle of the loaf. The dish towel Joan usually kept hanging over the handle on the refrigerator door lay half-chewed next to it. Priscilla cleaned up the bread, swept the floor, and put the dish towel in the trash. Then she took the vacuum cleaner into the living room.

"I'm sorry," she said as she plugged in the vacuum. "Looks like she got into the kitchen too. Your bread and your dish towel are, um, not worth saving."

Sister was looking up at Joan with pure puppy adoration, but Joan frowned at her.

"That's very bad," she said, shaking her finger at the pup. "You ruined my pillow and my bread and my towel. That's bad."

Sister ducked her head, and Joan immediately melted.

"It's all right, sweetie." She cuddled the puppy close. "Okay now, we'd better go for a walk before you give me something else to be upset about." She gave Priscilla and Kitty a sheepish grin as she grabbed Sister's leash. "If you'll both excuse us, we're going out for a few minutes. Make yourselves at home."

Priscilla made quick work of vacuuming up the remains of the pillow stuffing, and then she and Kitty sat down at the kitchen table with the envelope from Miss Waterman.

"It doesn't feel like there's much in here," Kitty said as she opened it. "But it's more than I had before."

She pulled out a few letters—some she had written to her aunt, a couple that her mother had sent Katherine—and four Christmas cards. There was also a black-and-white photograph of a young woman and a man standing before the altar at a church, clearly on their wedding day.

"That's Aunt Katherine and Uncle Bert," Kitty said.

"He's the one who died in a plane crash the day you were born?" Priscilla asked, studying the photo. "Wasn't she pretty?"

"I always thought so. I have a copy of this same picture at home somewhere. It was in Mother's things." Kitty picked up the last item, another photograph. "This one's new to me, but that's Aunt Katherine too."

She handed the picture to Priscilla. It showed two women at some kind of public function. They were sitting at a large round table with a white tablecloth and a flower arrangement in the middle of it.

"Looks like a banquet of some kind. Judging by the clothes and hair, it must have been sometime in the sixties." Priscilla grinned. "Those are some beehives they both had back then."

"I know." Kitty giggled. "And those cat-eye glasses. Goodness. But they look like they're having a great time."

"Who's that with her? They look like they could be sisters."

Kitty frowned as she studied the photo. "I don't think she had a sister. I don't think she had any family at all. That's why she was close to our family after Bert died. That is, until her next husband moved her out here."

"What happened to him?"

"All I ever heard was that he had heart problems and died not long after they were married. But I guess Aunt Katherine was happy here by then. I don't think she ever came back to Kansas. Anyway, I don't know who this other woman is." She looked on the back of the picture. "Hmm. It says '1967 Annual Fund Raiser, American Heart Association.' It doesn't say who it is."

"What did we miss?" Joan asked when she and Sister came back inside. "Anything interesting?" She sat down with them at the kitchen table, and the puppy immediately flopped down at her feet.

"Only some letters and things," Priscilla said, "and a couple of pictures."

Kitty handed her the picture from the fund raiser. "That's my aunt Katherine, but I don't know who the other woman is."

Joan looked at it for a moment and then smiled. "Well, well. I'm pretty sure that's Miss Caroline Waterman herself."

"No." Priscilla took the picture from her, looking at it more closely than she had before. "Really? But how do you know? She never goes out."

"That wasn't until later," Joan said. "Not until about twenty years ago. I always assumed it was because she wasn't in good health, but from what you tell me about her relationship with her family, it sounds like that wasn't it at all. Anyway, even before then, she wasn't much for being out and about all the time, but she did do charity events once in a while. I remember that from when I was still in school. She was on the local news sometimes, like when she made a huge donation to the library." Joan shook her head, still studying the picture. "Boy, that was a long time ago. I wonder what she looks like now."

"The same, I'd guess," Priscilla said. "Just older."

Kitty's full lips turned down. "Too bad we can't see for ourselves. I'd still like to thank her, but I guess I'll have to be satisfied with this." She put everything back into the envelope. "It's sure not much."

Priscilla smiled sympathetically and then noticed Sister was sound asleep with her head on Joan's foot. "Maybe we'd better get going. It looks like it's naptime here."

Joan looked down and laughed softly. "Poor baby. I think she's had a busy day."

"Tell me the truth," Priscilla said seriously. "Has she been a lot of trouble?"

"Oh, you know how it is." Joan shrugged. "There's always a period of adjustment. For the dog and the human."

"I'm sorry about your bread."

That made Joan laugh. "I can buy some more. I sure didn't think she'd be able to get up on the counter in here, though."

"I bet she jumped up on that chair in the corner," Kitty said. "It's still a jump to get to the counter, especially for a little one like her, but I bet that's how she did it."

Joan exhaled heavily. "I'll just have to do more puppy-proofing."

"Let me know if I can help," Priscilla said, standing. "And make sure you latch that crate good and tight."

Joan and Kitty stood too. Sister made a soft little whimper when Joan moved her foot, but her sleep didn't seem to be otherwise disturbed.

"Don't worry," Joan assured Priscilla. "Thank you for the lunch, Kitty. It was delicious. And thanks for letting me tag along today. It's certainly been interesting."

"You're very welcome," Kitty said. "Thank you for identifying Miss Waterman for me." She shook the envelope. "I wish there had been more in here, but I guess after over two years, Miss Waterman didn't see much reason to keep a lot of Aunt Katherine's stuff."

"At least you don't have to worry about your aunt anymore," Joan said as she walked them to the door. "Do you think you'll be staying much longer?"

"Probably not." Kitty sighed. "I guess I've found out everything there is to know."

"Your flight's not till tomorrow," Priscilla said, "so we have a little more time, unless you decide to stay longer. You can help me some more with my museum, and I think you'd love to go to church with us."

"Do your cousins all go too?"

"Well, Joan and Gail and her father, Uncle Hugh, go to my church, Faith Fellowship. Trudy and her husband, Dan, go to Grace Community. I think you'd enjoy the service, and I think the choir is having some special music tomorrow, so I'm sure that will be good. Oh, and Gerald, the guy we saw at the pet store yesterday, goes there too."

Priscilla knew that last comment was a mistake the moment it left her mouth. Kitty looked mischievous, and Joan was definitely hiding a giggle.

"Well?" Priscilla asked, pretending to be stern.

"You're stuck with me at least until tomorrow afternoon, but I really need to get back to real life after that. Keith'll think I've left him," Kitty said.

Priscilla chuckled. "You call him every day. I don't think he's the least bit worried about that. Come on, if we're going. I'd like to stop by the historical museum, just to get a few ideas."

"Ooh, I'd love to see that." Kitty turned to Joan. "Thanks for letting us stop in. You take care of Sister. She's a sweetie."

Priscilla and Kitty spent most of the afternoon in the East Shore Historical Museum. Priscilla enjoyed showing her friend through the familiar exhibits, glad to be able to talk about them as if she were an expert on life in Martha's Vineyard. She also got to introduce Kitty to Mildred Pearson, the museum's curator, and they spent an entertaining but unproductive few minutes talking about the break-in at the Cavanaugh Museum. Other than expressing her shock at the incident and her dismay at the loss of the irreplaceable items that had been on display there, Mildred's only advice was for Priscilla to make sure the locks on the lighthouse were sturdy.

When Priscilla and Kitty got back to the cottage, there was a familiar black Lamborghini parked in the street out front.

"What's he doing here?" Kitty asked, wide-eyed.

Priscilla didn't like the idea of him knowing where she lived, though she wasn't quite sure why it should bother her. "I guess we're about to find out."

She parked the SUV in the gravel drive rather than the garage. The instant she turned off the engine, Rowan Cavanaugh popped out of his car and came striding up the drive.

"Mrs. Grant." He stuck out his hand, his smile wide. "I hope you don't mind my dropping by unannounced, but I've been trying to keep my visit to the island as casual as possible. You know how it is—reporters and constituents and staff. It can get to be a little much sometimes."

"Of course." Priscilla shook his hand. She didn't at all know how that was, and she didn't want to.

"I like to get out on my own from time to time. You know, be a simple, private citizen without all the bother. But I thought, while I was here, I'd see if Mrs. Merrick had a moment to talk to me." He shook Kitty's hand too, and his smile broadened. "Would it be possible for me to visit with you both for a few minutes? I promise I won't take much of your time."

Priscilla looked at Kitty, who gave her a subtle shrug in return.

"If you like," Priscilla said. "For a few minutes. I'm not exactly prepared for company."

"Nonsense," Cavanaugh said. "I bet you're the type of woman whose home is always tidy and orderly. I have an instinct about these things."

Or he asked someone about me. Priscilla gave him the slightest nod. "I'll be right with you, as soon as I let my dog out."

"Not a problem. I'm in no hurry."

Priscilla led him and Kitty to the cottage and unlocked the door. As she expected, Jake was waiting to go out. He looked warily at the new visitor but did no more than watch as Cavanaugh walked to the sofa and took a seat. Kitty took the chair next to him, which meant that, when Priscilla got back from letting Jake out, she would have no choice but to sit on the couch too.

Once she had let Jake outside, she prepared a tray with fresh coffee and the oatmeal cookies she and Kitty had baked the night before. She wondered while she was busy getting the refreshments what Kitty would find to talk about, but it was fairly obvious as soon as she entered the living room that Cavanaugh had almost exclusively carried the conversation.

"I was telling Mrs. Merrick how long my family's been on Martha's Vineyard. Of course, my headquarters are in Boston and I have to be gadding all over the country these days, but I always think of this as home." He reached over and gave Kitty's hand a patronizing pat. "You know, it is fascinating to find someone who knew my grandmother's personal maid. As I said before, Grandmother was very fond of your aunt Katherine. I would have loved to speak to Mrs. Evans myself, to hear her memories of Grandmother, but obviously that's not possible."

"No," Kitty said. "I really wanted to see her too. And, I guess, for a lot of the same reasons. She would have had memories of my mother from when they were both young. I wish now I had asked her to tell me more. Mother told me that Katherine worked for Rosie Cavanaugh, but that didn't mean much to me when I was a little girl. I just knew she worked for a rich lady out east."

"That is a shame," Cavanaugh said. "Between the Cavanaughs and the Watermans, I'm sure she must have told your mother some interesting tales."

"Not that I ever heard. I don't think Aunt Katherine was much for gossip. She always said that if you couldn't say anything nice about somebody, you shouldn't say anything at all."

Cavanaugh nodded thoughtfully. "You know, it would be a better world if everyone thought the same." He glanced at Priscilla and then turned, smiling, to Kitty again. "So she never sent you anything? A family album or a book or anything like that."

"No. But that was all a little before my time. I'm sorry."

"She never sent anything to your mother either?"

"Mother never told me about it if she did," Kitty told him, "and I didn't find anything when I went through her things after she died."

"Well, I just thought I'd ask," Cavanaugh said, his smile broader than ever. "You know how it is. When you're young, the past doesn't mean much. Eventually, though, you want to know as much as you can about what makes you you."

"That's what makes museums like Malcolm's so interesting. It's too bad what happened with the break-in and everything." Priscilla watched his eyes. "I'd hate for the museum to go away altogether. Do you think you might open one yourself? People are always interested in the Cavanaughs."

"Well, I don't know," Cavanaugh said. "The Waterman family took good care of the things we loaned them, and there are a lot of other interesting items we could add from our personal memen-tos. You know, I might consider doing exactly that. I'm just glad the things we loaned Mr. Waterman were retrieved in time."

"That was a lucky break," Priscilla said. "Pretty amazing, as a matter of fact, that you got your things back right in the nick of time."

"I knew the museum was closing, and I thought it was as good a time as any to take back my property," Cavanaugh replied, his expression cool. "I hope you're not implying anything else."

Kitty looked on, her dark eyes round.

"No," Priscilla said, reminding herself that she had no evidence of anything at all.

"If you'll be so good as to remember, I offered to buy those things from Waterman. He could have had almost any price he cared to name."

"But he didn't." Priscilla forced herself to keep an even tone. "He simply didn't want to sell, for whatever reasons he might have. Not everything has a price, Mr. Cavanaugh."

"I realize that. I'm pretty sure I realize that much more than you do."

For a minute, there was only taut silence.

Finally, Kitty cleared her throat. "I wish there was something more I could tell you, Mr. Cavanaugh. I just don't know anything about it."

He flashed her his politician smile again. "I suppose it was a long shot, Mrs. Merrick, but I had to give it the old college try, eh?"

She nodded. "Sure."

"Though I, uh, I understand Miss Waterman sent you a few of your aunt's things. Things she'd left behind in the house when she died."

Again, Kitty nodded.

Priscilla narrowed her eyes. "How do you know about that?"

Cavanaugh shrugged. "I hear things here and there. Talk to people. They're usually quite helpful when they realize how appreciative I can be."

You mean when you pay them off, Priscilla thought. "You talked to Miss Waterman's housekeeper. She's the only one besides us and Miss Waterman who knew about these things."

He nodded serenely. "Do you think I might see them?"

Kitty glanced at Priscilla.

"They're yours now," Priscilla told her. "You can do what you want with them."

Cavanaugh was looking exceptionally oily right then, and Priscilla was hoping Kitty would tell him to take a hike, but after a moment of uncertainty, she handed him the envelope.

"There's really not much to see," she said. "To be honest, I was kind of disappointed that this is all there was."

He glanced at the photos and scanned the cards and letters. Then he put everything back into the envelope and returned it to Kitty. "That is disappointing." His jovial expression became more intense. "And there wasn't anything else? Anything at all?" His dark eyes glittered. "I like to think of you ladies as my friends. We Cavanaughs are always good to our friends."

He didn't say more, but the implication of what that meant regarding his enemies was clear.

"There wasn't anything else," Kitty restated.

"You didn't leave anything in the SUV? Or at Mrs. Abernathy's house?"

Priscilla tightened her lips. How did he know they had been at Joan's? "Just what are you looking for, Mr. Cavanaugh?"

He exhaled, smiling again. "As I said, I merely want to know more about my family, especially my grandmother. I thought Mrs. Evans might have left behind something pertaining to her. But it may be that I simply have to be satisfied with what I have already."

"I don't know about that," Priscilla said, standing. "But I know if there *is* anything else, we don't have a clue what it is or where it is."

Kitty smiled apologetically. "Aunt Katherine really didn't have much. Evidently, what's in that envelope is all Miss Waterman kept of hers."

Cavanaugh stood too, taking the hint. "It was good of you to show me what you had. Thank you." He nodded to Priscilla. "Mrs. Grant."

CHAPTER EIGHT

Priscilla escorted Cavanaugh to the door and then peeped through the blinds as he walked down the drive to his car.

"Why am I not surprised?" she huffed, and Kitty hurried over to look out the window too.

"What? What did he do?"

"He tried to pretend he wasn't, but I swear he was looking into my car as he walked by. You know he wanted to see if we left anything of your aunt's in there."

"You don't think he'd try to break in or anything, do you?" Kitty asked.

"I'm glad I don't leave a bunch of stuff in my car all the time. Since he did look, he knows now that there's nothing in there. At least I hope so. I'll put the car in the garage in a little while. Just in case."

Jake came up to the window, trying to figure out what was so interesting, and Priscilla patted him on the head. "It's all right, boy. He's gone now."

They sat on the couch again, and Priscilla was glad to have Jake snuggled right beside her. "I don't care what he says, he's after something specific. I'd sure like to know what it is."

"But we told him the truth," Kitty said. "Whatever it is, we don't have it."

"But does he believe that? I'm wondering now if we shouldn't tell the police what we overheard when he and Malcolm were having their little discussion."

"I don't know," Kitty said, a little quiver in her voice.

Priscilla lifted her chin. "You're not going to let that blowhard scare you, are you?" Maybe she was talking to herself more than to Kitty.

"No. But he makes me nervous. And he makes me wonder how Aunt Katherine might have been involved with all this. Do you think she stole something from his family? I can't believe she would ever do that."

"You would know her better than I do." Priscilla stroked Jake's head, thinking. "Maybe it's not something she stole but something that was given to her. If she and Rosie Cavanaugh were such good friends, Rosie might have given her something. A keepsake or memento."

Kitty didn't reply at first, but then she took a startled breath. "Do you think it could have been something she sold or loaned to Malcolm's museum? Maybe that's why Mr. Cavanaugh was so eager to buy everything."

"Or he thought she did. But what could it have been? If it was a valuable of some kind, he was willing to pay for it. It sounds like he was willing to pay well over what it was worth to get it back. Why didn't he come right out and say what he's after? And I guess we're back to the question of why Malcolm didn't want to sell. Unless he thought he could make more off of it by making it public."

Again, Kitty didn't answer right away. "Do you really think some of the things in the museum were fakes?"

Priscilla frowned. "I don't know for sure. I didn't get to see much, and maybe I was wrong about that campaign ribbon. I guess we'll never know now." She couldn't hold back a bit of a giggle. "If Cavanaugh *was* actually behind the break-in, he can't complain to the police about ending up with counterfeits."

Kitty's worried expression didn't change. "But what does all of this have to do with Aunt Katherine?" Her big eyes got bigger. "You don't think it might have been something she *knew* rather than something she had, do you?"

Priscilla didn't like that thought. Not one little bit. "But she's dead. If she did know something, she can never tell anyone now."

"But she could have written to someone or maybe even had one of Rosie Cavanaugh's letters. There were a lot of letters in the museum before it was robbed."

"But they were sitting out in plain sight," Priscilla reminded her. "If there was some kind of sensitive information in one of them, it would be old news by now, wouldn't it?"

"I suppose."

"Cavanaugh sure seems to be looking for something in partic-ular. If it was in the museum and he's behind the break-in, he has it now. Or maybe," Priscilla considered, "it's because he *was* behind the break-in that he just now realizes that nothing in the museum is what he was looking for."

"But how does that tie in to the counterfeit items? I mean, if they were counterfeit in the first place."

Priscilla could only shake her head. "And you're sure your aunt never sent you anything to do with the Cavanaughs?"

"Never. Even if she did, I don't remember seeing anything, and I haven't kept anything that mentions them. I know that for sure. What could it be?"

Priscilla didn't particularly like what she was thinking right now. Maybe she shouldn't bring it up.

"We don't have much to go on," she said finally, "but I'd like to know what's really happening here. If Cavanaugh wasn't behind the museum break-in, who was? And if he was, why does he think it has something to do with your aunt?"

"He scares me a little," Kitty said. "Maybe I'm making more of it than I should, but he does."

"Me too," Priscilla admitted, "but we're not going to be bullied by Rowan Cavanaugh IV or anyone else, okay?"

"Okay," Kitty said, very subdued.

"What are you thinking?" Priscilla asked when she didn't say anything else.

Kitty only shook her head.

"Come on, tell me."

Kitty took a deep breath. "Okay, I know this is going to sound silly, but what if Aunt Katherine didn't die two years ago? What if she's hiding because she knows something about Rosie Cavanaugh the family wouldn't want getting out, and she's afraid they might do something to her if they knew, and now Mr. Cavanaugh is looking for her."

"I don't think it sounds silly," Priscilla said. "I mean, yeah, it sounds really unlikely, but I was kind of wondering the same thing."

"I'm still not sure I buy Miss Waterman's explanation about the letters. Maybe, if she and Aunt Katherine were as good of friends as everybody says, she's the one who helped her disappear." Kitty's expression brightened. "Maybe Aunt Katherine did write those letters after all."

"Well, that would explain the letters but not the autopsy, the coroner's report, or the death certificate. And it wouldn't explain why she suddenly stopped writing to you."

Kitty's full lips turned down. "Couldn't all those things be faked? I mean, with someone as powerful and connected as Rowan Cavanaugh—"

"But, theoretically at least, she's hiding *from* him, not being hidden *by* him, so whatever strings he could possibly pull don't really enter into the question. And though Miss Waterman is something of a personage around here, she doesn't have that kind of power. At least I don't think so. It would mean that everyone from the coroner to the funeral home to the EMTs who allegedly came out to the house the night your aunt fell would have to be in on it. That's a lot of people to pay off and keep quiet for the rest of their lives, don't you think?"

"I guess." Kitty sighed. "Still, couldn't the police check it out? Miss Waterman is such a recluse and that housekeeper of hers is so determined to keep everybody away. Isn't there at least a possibility that Aunt Katherine is still alive and hiding there?"

"Kitty—"

"It's possible, isn't it?"

Priscilla shook her head, smiling faintly. "I suppose it might have happened like that. But the police already went out to talk to Miss Waterman. They didn't find anything suspicious."

"Because Aunt Katherine is hiding. What do you think she'd do if the police came to the door? Sit on the couch and wave?"

"Okay, let's assume she's in hiding, there or somewhere else. If Mr. Cavanaugh thinks she died over two years ago, why is he looking for her now? Why is he only now trying to get Malcolm to sell him whatever was in the museum?"

"Maybe he didn't find out about it, whatever is incriminating, until recently," Kitty said.

"Then why did your aunt go into hiding over two years ago?"

Kitty twisted her fingers together, thinking. "Because she *thought* he was going to come after her?"

"Why then and not twenty years ago? Or thirty? Or forty?" Priscilla asked. "If she did find out something or have possession of something that might be damaging to the Cavanaugh family, it had to have been while she was still working for them. Why wouldn't she have gone into hiding then, if she thought he would be after her someday? Why fifty-something years later?"

Kitty exhaled heavily. "I guess it doesn't make sense, but something's going on, don't you think?"

"Mr. Cavanaugh is certainly after something, and it's something he wants very badly." Priscilla thought for a while. "Do you mind if I look at that note you got from Miss Waterman one more time?"

Looking puzzled, Kitty handed her the whole envelope.

Priscilla opened it and pulled out the note. "Who's the only person besides the housekeeper who's seen Miss Waterman in the past twenty years?"

Kitty shrugged.

"From what everyone says, it's her attorney." Priscilla read from the note. "'Paul J. Edison, Attorney at Law.' The address is on Franklin. If he's come to the house to take care of her business affairs for twenty years, he has to have met your aunt more than once."

Kitty's face lit up. "Then he ought to know something about her. Maybe he saw her shortly before she died." She gave Priscilla a sly look. "*If* she died."

Priscilla chuckled. "Okay, but his office won't be open until Monday. That means you're going to have to cancel your flight for tomorrow afternoon and square things with your boss and your client and your husband. Is that going to be all right?"

Kitty considered for a moment. "It's going to have to be. There's something about all this that bothers me, and I don't think I can just leave until I find out more. You don't mind my staying on, do you? There is some work I need to take care of, but I think I can handle it from here, as long as I'm back in time for my big closing."

"You're more than welcome. Now, you make whatever calls you need to, and I'll go see what I've got grocery-wise to get us through the weekend."

"Okay," Kitty said, "as long as you let me buy whatever we need. And maybe a few treats." Jake's head lifted at the word *treats*, and Kitty roughed up the fur on top of his head. "Some for you too, if that's okay with your mom."

Priscilla smiled. "It's a deal."

They went to the Stop&Shop and got a few things to carry them through the first part of the week, a variety of human and canine treats included. Then they spent the remainder of the afternoon working on the lighthouse museum and suggesting and discarding various theories about what might have happened to Katherine Evans and what Rowan Cavanaugh was looking for. Only the museum work ended up being very productive.

After Kitty cooked them what her husband called her world-famous meatloaf, a delicious ground-beef concoction stuffed full of cheese and vegetables, they spent the rest of Saturday night watching William Powell and Myrna Loy in *The Thin Man* and *After the Thin Man*. It was a relaxing evening, and it was good to put their questions about Katherine Evans's death on the back burner for a while.

As Priscilla had hoped, the music at Faith Fellowship Church the next morning was wonderful. The choir sang a lovely a cappella version of "My Jesus, I Love Thee" that touched not only the ear but the soul as well. But she couldn't help exchanging incredulous glances with Kitty when the text for the sermon turned out to be Matthew 10:26: "...for there is nothing covered, that shall not be revealed; and hid, that shall not be known."

Show us, Lord, she prayed silently as the pastor preached the message. *If there is something hidden that should be brought to light, help us find out what it is. And keep us safe as we look. Give us courage, and let us not be afraid to do whatever it is that You want us to do.*

She noticed Kitty's eyes were closed and wondered if she was praying the same prayer.

After the service, she and Kitty, along with Joan, Gail, Uncle Hugh, and Gerald, met up with Trudy and Dan at the Colonial Inn for lunch. The eight of them were too many for Gerald's usual booth, but Hilda seated them at a large table in the center of the restaurant. The food and the company were both excellent. When they were all full and mostly talked out, Gerald asked Kitty if she had seen much of the island.

"Not really," Kitty said. "Mostly we've been—"

"She's been helping me with the lighthouse museum," Priscilla said, not wanting Kitty to say anything about the Cavanaughs or the Watermans in public. "I thought it would be nice for us to do nothing but have fun today."

"What did you have in mind?" Gail asked.

Everyone looked at Kitty, and she turned a little pink. "I don't know, really. Almost anything would be interesting." She paused for a second. "There is one thing I'd like to see while I'm here." She paused again, looking uncertain.

"What?" Priscilla asked. "Is it something that would be open on a Sunday?"

"I think so. Maybe. And I don't think it's very far from here."

Everyone looked at her expectantly.

"Well, I heard that Oak Bluffs has some wonderful little cottages to see and a flea market and even a carousel."

Dan looked pained, and Trudy elbowed him. "I think it would be fun!" she said. "I haven't been out that way in ages. Not for the touristy stuff, anyway. What do you girls think?"

"The market probably won't be open yet." Gail's gray-blue eyes were warm. "I don't think it gets going till next month. But there are some shops and things, and the carousel. It's really old-fashioned, though. Nothing high tech."

"But that's what makes it so lovely," Kitty said. "It's been the same for over a hundred years."

"Not quite the same," Joan said. "They've painted and spruced it up over time. But they've kept the original style. The horses have real horsehair manes and tails. It's really pretty."

"We could go to Ben and Bill's," Gail put in. "I mean, for a treat later on."

Kitty raised her eyebrows. "Ben and Bill? Who are they?"

"They sell some very excellent chocolates," Priscilla told her. "So what do you think? Shall we give it a try?"

Dan and Gerald immediately made up some reasonably convincing excuses for why they couldn't come along. Hugh was much more straightforward.

"Whatever you girls want to do is fine," he said, lifting his bushy white eyebrows, "as long as you take me home first. I've been to Oak Bluffs more than once in my time, and I'd rather have my nap."

"All right, Pop," Gail said. "I'll drop you back at home. Looks like it'll be just us girls."

"While you're doing that, I'm going to take Sister for a little walk." Joan looked at her watch. "I don't want to have any more accidents."

"She hasn't been too much trouble, has she?" Priscilla asked.

Trudy and Gail looked at each other but didn't say anything.

Joan only shrugged. "Just puppy stuff. It's fine. But we probably ought to get going."

As Priscilla had expected, Oak Bluffs wasn't quite the bustling place it was during the summer season, but the five of them had fun. Priscilla especially enjoyed seeing Kitty's pleasure in the new-to-her sights. She enjoyed the shops and the cottages and seemed especially enchanted by the old-fashioned carousel. It wasn't large or particularly unusual, but it was the oldest one in the country and had been lovingly restored. There was something relaxing and nostalgic about riding on it to the sound of vintage tunes played on a Wurlitzer band organ and trying for the elusive brass ring.

Afterward, chatting and laughing like a group of schoolgirls, they walked down Circuit Avenue toward Ben and Bill's Chocolate Emporium.

"You'll have to come back one summer," Priscilla told Kitty as they looked into the windows of the shops that were closed on Sunday afternoon. "Then you can really—"

She stopped when she saw a black Lamborghini turn the corner ahead of them and then speed away.

CHAPTER NINE

The Lamborghini was too far off for Priscilla to read the license plate, so she couldn't really be sure whose it was, but surely there weren't that many of them on the island.

"You saw it too," Kitty said, her face suddenly pale. "But why would he be in Oak Bluffs? Especially on a Sunday?"

"Maybe that's why," Priscilla said, quickly grabbing Kitty's arm and turning with her toward one of the shop windows. "Don't let her see you," she whispered.

Reflected in the glass, she could clearly see a woman hurry across the street and get into a late-model Cadillac Eldorado. It was Anna Vaden.

"What's she doing here too?" Kitty breathed.

"Wait," Priscilla told her, still watching in the glass, but Anna quickly drove away, back toward Tisbury.

"Who was that?" Gail demanded once she was gone. "What is going on?"

"That's Miss Waterman's housekeeper," Priscilla said. "The one with the guard dog."

The cousins gaped at her.

Priscilla looked up and down the street, but it was clear now. "And that black Lamborghini we saw belongs to Rowan Cavanaugh IV. I'm sure of it."

"You think he was here to see Anna?" Gail asked. "Why would he be?"

Priscilla shook her head. "This just gets more suspicious all the time..."

"Maybe he was talking to her about what my aunt left behind at Miss Waterman's house," Kitty suggested. "She had to be the one who told him that we were asking about it in the first place."

"But why here? Why not at Miss Waterman's or at least in Tisbury?" Priscilla scanned the street again, just to be sure neither of them was coming back. "If he thinks something of his grandmother's is at the house, he'd have to deal with Miss Waterman herself, wouldn't he?"

"Not if this housekeeper is doing a bit of independent contracting." Joan pursed her lips. "If Cavanaugh went to the house and told her what he wanted, maybe she agreed to look around and let him know what she found. Miss Waterman probably doesn't have a clue what all is in that big old house by now. Maybe she doesn't get around so well anymore. Didn't you say April said Miss Waterman wasn't feeling well when she went by there the other day?"

"That's what she told me," Priscilla said. "I'd hate to think someone would steal from an elderly lady like that, but I guess it happens all the time. If that's what Anna Vaden has been doing, she must have done a lot of it. Did you see that car she was driving?"

Joan bobbed her head, bright-eyed as a sparrow. "I can't see a housekeeper being able to afford something like that, not even working for someone like Miss Waterman."

"Maybe it's Miss Waterman's, and she just uses it," Kitty said. "I know Aunt Katherine didn't have a car, and she did all the errands for Miss Waterman."

"Could be," Priscilla agreed, "and it could be she borrowed those designer shoes and those diamond earrings too. But you remember that picture of Miss Waterman and your aunt, right? They were both very small women, very delicate. Even if Miss Waterman put on a lot of weight over the years, Anna would never be able to fit into her shoes. She's too big-boned."

"She's stealing from Miss Waterman!" Trudy gasped, her curly hair bouncing as she looked from Priscilla and then to Kitty and back again. "That's awful! That's just not right!"

"Keep your voice down," Joan told her, putting a calming hand on her sister's arm. "We don't know that. Maybe it's something else entirely."

"I'm just wondering if it has more to do with Mr. Cavanaugh than Miss Waterman," Priscilla said.

"Even if he did pay her for something she found in the house, I can't imagine some keepsake of his grandmother's would be worth that kind of money," Gail said.

Priscilla raised one eyebrow. "It depends on whether it's something he wants to keep or wants to get rid of."

"But why would he pay for something he wanted to get rid of?" Trudy asked.

"He didn't look to me like someone who just wanted to collect his family mementos," Priscilla said. "He seemed too urgent for that."

"And very specific," Kitty mused. "Like he's looking for something in particular."

"Exactly. And it could be proof of something he wants hushed up."

"Something he's willing to pay handsomely for," Gail added.

"But if that was the case," Joan said, "how could the housekeeper have the car and the shoes and the jewelry already if he's just paying her off now?"

Priscilla frowned. She hadn't quite thought that through. "I guess that wouldn't make sense. Unless he's been doing it for a long time." She thought a bit longer. "But if that's the case, why is he here now? Why didn't he try to buy up everything from Malcolm's museum years ago? If it was something he just found out about, something incriminating, he would have had no reason to pay off Anna Vaden in the past."

"If she *is* being paid off," Trudy added, "and not just stealing things and selling them."

"Now we're right back where we started," Gail said with a sigh. "Let's go to Ben and Bill's."

They continued their discussion as they walked up the street and for the remainder of their stay in Oak Bluffs, but even gourmet chocolates didn't seem to clarify matters. By the time Priscilla dropped her cousins off at their homes, she still had more questions than answers about Kitty's aunt and how she fit into whatever was going on at the Waterman house and with Rowan Cavanaugh. She decided that the only thing to do was go see the one person besides

Anna Vaden who had been inside the Waterman house while Katherine Evans was still alive.

On Monday morning, Priscilla and Kitty visited the offices of Paul J. Edison, Attorney at Law, which were located in an old, tree-shaded Victorian house on Franklin Street. The inside was nicely decorated but not ostentatious and, over the fireplace, featured a large framed print showing the Founding Fathers signing the Constitution.

The secretary, a short, chubby woman with graying hair and glasses, told Priscilla and Kitty that Mr. Edison was still in with clients but would be with them shortly. She brought them coffee and then went back to her keyboard.

"She's very fast," Kitty whispered once they had listened to a minute or two of the constant tapping from the secretary's desk.

"From what I hear," Priscilla whispered back, "in this job, you have to be."

An elderly couple came from the back of the office followed by a tall young man with horn-rimmed glasses and a Beatles haircut.

"We'll have everything ready for you to sign by Friday," the young man said. "If you'll just tell Dorothy here what time will be convenient for you, we'll get you all squared away."

The couple thanked him and turned to the secretary.

"Come right this way," Dorothy said, "and we'll set up a time. Mr. Edison, Mrs. Grant and Mrs. Merrick are here."

Mr. Edison smiled at Priscilla and Kitty. "Come on into my office."

He led them down a little hallway, past more framed copies of historic legal documents and one rather impressive painting of an American eagle, and finally into the messiest office Priscilla had ever seen. It was quite a contrast to the neatly maintained reception area.

"Dorothy hates it in here," Mr. Edison said, removing a file folder from one of the two chairs in front of his overburdened desk. "But I know exactly where everything is." He sat down, almost but not quite blocked from their view by a precarious stack of books and papers. "Now, what can I do for you? I understand from when you made this appointment that this is somehow connected with Miss Waterman. Is that right?"

"Sort of," Kitty said. "It's kind of a long story."

"Take your time," Mr. Edison said with a smile that made him look even younger than before. He must have been in his thirties, though he certainly didn't look it.

"Well, as you know, my name is Kitty Merrick. My mother's sister-in-law and best friend was Katherine Evans. She used to be Miss Waterman's housekeeper."

Mr. Edison nodded, taking notes on a yellow legal pad.

"I—I guess I must have misunderstood," Kitty continued, "because I thought you had been Miss Waterman's lawyer for a long time, like thirty or forty years, but that can't possibly be right."

"You must be thinking of Mr. Barnes," Mr. Edison said. "I believe he handled Miss Waterman's affairs from 1972 until he retired to Florida three years ago. I've been taking care of her ever since. Of course, you realize I can't discuss anything to do with one of my clients without that client's permission."

"Oh, we didn't come here to ask anything like that," Priscilla assured him. "Nothing about Miss Waterman."

"We just thought you might be able to tell us something about my aunt Katherine," Kitty said. She looked the young man over again. "But maybe not."

"I'm afraid you're right," he said. "The only housekeeper I've ever seen at Miss Waterman's is Ms. Vaden. I remember Mr. Barnes talking about going to see Miss Waterman and mentioning Katherine, her housekeeper. I just assumed she had retired. He said she and Miss Waterman were about the same age."

"And you never met my aunt," Kitty said with a sigh.

"I'm sorry, no. I couldn't tell you anything about her at all."

"Would it be possible for us to contact Mr. Barnes?" Priscilla asked. "All we're looking for is someone who remembers her, who might be able to tell Kitty how she was doing when he last saw her."

"You can't get in touch with your aunt yourself?" Mr. Edison asked Kitty.

Kitty shook her head. "Evidently she passed away more than two years ago. It seemed so strange, so I'd really like to know more."

"I see." Mr. Edison smiled faintly. "And, of course, Miss Waterman won't see you. Have you gone to the house?"

"A few times," Priscilla said. "The housekeeper was good enough to take Miss Waterman a couple of messages, and

Miss Waterman sent down an envelope that contained some of the letters and photos Kitty's aunt had left behind, but she wouldn't see us. That's why we thought we'd come see her attorney, but obviously you're not who we really want to see. Is there any way we could get Mr. Barnes's contact information?"

"I'm sorry," Mr. Edison told them. "I mean, I could give it to you, but it wouldn't do you any good. He's in Alzheimer's care down in Tampa Bay. That's why he had to retire suddenly three years ago. We had a struggle to get the office straightened out after that, but we did." He glanced at the mess surrounding them and grinned. "As regards the cases, anyway."

Kitty frowned. "And nobody else ever went to Miss Waterman's house but him?"

"I'm sorry. No, not that I ever heard of. They say she got very reclusive about twenty years ago, and I'm afraid that was before my time."

Priscilla knit her brows. "But if you took over for Mr. Barnes three years ago, wouldn't you have met Katherine Evans when he took you to introduce you to Miss Waterman?"

Mr. Edison shook his head. "We talked about his introducing me to her, seeing as she was so very particular about whom she actually saw from day to day, but then Mr. Barnes became very ill. He had heart problems, which they found out were brought on by some of the medications he was taking and which made his Alzheimer's dramatically worse too. By the time the doctors had everything figured out, he was really in no condition to do anything business-related. I decided it wouldn't do any good to worry him over Miss Waterman. I just waited until she called to speak to him and then explained why he was no longer available."

"What did she say?" Kitty asked.

"She was very nice about it. Mr. Barnes always said she was a gracious lady, even if she was set in her ways and very stubborn at times. I told her I would understand if she wanted to deal with someone else. I figured she'd want someone with more experience." Mr. Edison grinned again, looking more boyish than ever. "I've been in practice for several years now, but that's nothing compared to how long Mr. Barnes was taking care of things for her."

Priscilla smiled at him. "But she didn't object."

"Surprisingly, she didn't. She said she was sure that Mr. Barnes had told me what I needed to know about her affairs and that there were good records in our files. She was right about that. Everything has gone smoothly since I took over, and I think she would tell you the same."

"And when did you finally meet her?" Priscilla asked.

"I don't remember. A few months later. I had expected her to call before then, but she didn't. I suppose she didn't have any need of legal counsel until that time."

Kitty looked at Priscilla. "I guess that's all, then." She stood up. "Thank you, Mr. Edison. We're sorry to have taken up your time."

He stood too and came around the desk to shake hands with both of them. "It's no problem at all. I'm sorry I couldn't tell you anything about your aunt."

Kitty was silent during the ride back to Priscilla's cottage. Priscilla was disappointed herself at not finding out anything at all from the lawyer, but she also wanted to let Kitty deal with her emotions in her own way without intruding on them.

"I'm sorry," Kitty said as they pulled up in the driveway.

Priscilla glanced over at her. "For what?"

"I can't go home yet. I know there's something going on here, and Aunt Katherine's right in the middle of it."

"I feel the same way, but all we're hitting is dead ends. What else can we do?"

Kitty shrugged and again was silent. They went into the cottage, and Priscilla was about to take Jake for his walk when Kitty spoke again.

"Why do you suppose Miss Waterman is selling her property now?" she asked.

"I can tell you have something on your mind," Priscilla said. "What is it?"

"I don't know." Kitty perched on the couch as if she meant to jump up again at any second. "I was just thinking that if Anna was getting money from somewhere and it wasn't Mr. Cavanaugh, who else could it be? Who else might have been paying her off, not just recently but for a long time?"

"You don't mean Miss Waterman, do you?" Priscilla gripped the leash a little more tightly as Jake tugged at it, eager to go out. "Why?"

"Why is she suddenly so eager to sell that property?" Kitty asked. "Why now, when everybody says she wanted to keep it the way it is forever? Why does she want to close the museum when she told her nephew for years that she didn't want to sell?"

Priscilla perched on the arm of the couch, ignoring Jake's pleading look. "Okay, suppose Anna is blackmailing Miss Waterman. Why? She hasn't left the house for twenty years. Anna's been there only since your aunt died, so two and a half years, more or less. What could an eighty-something-year-old woman have done in her own home that someone could bleed her dry for? If she's selling the property and the museum, she must have used almost all of whatever liquid assets she had until now. And, if rumor is true, there were a lot of liquid assets."

"Right. And Mr. Cavanaugh really wants to find something that has to do with his grandmother. I asked this before, but what if it's something someone knows rather than something someone has?"

"You're not going back to that idea that your aunt is in hiding somewhere and her death was faked, are you? Who would have faked it? Where would she be hiding?"

"I don't know," Kitty admitted. "But what if that's what Anna is blackmailing Miss Waterman over? Everybody says she and Aunt Katherine were great friends. The only friend either of them had. What if Anna found out where Katherine is, and Miss Waterman is paying her to keep quiet because Mr. Cavanaugh would want to shut her up forever if he could find her?"

"Then what was Anna talking to Cavanaugh about in Oak Bluffs?"

Kitty bit her lip. "Maybe she knows Miss Waterman is running out of money and she's negotiating with Mr. Cavanaugh to see what he would pay to find out where Aunt Katherine is. I don't know if changing allegiances like that would bother her."

"I don't think it would bother her at all," Priscilla said, her mouth tightening. "But I still think that's a pretty far-fetched story. There'd have to be a lot of people involved, and it's not easy keeping a secret like that."

"But maybe that's why Miss Waterman is running out of money so fast." Kitty's eyes were suddenly bright. "Think about it. She'd have a whole lot of people to pay off and not just small amounts. That could be why Anna is willing to talk to Mr. Cavanaugh now. The money is running out. That's why she has to sell her property and the museum house."

"Okay, then how does any of that fit in with the museum burglary?" Priscilla asked as Jake nudged her hand with his wet nose, reminding her that they were supposed to go for a walk. "Just one more minute, boy."

"I'll keep thinking." Kitty smiled at them. "You two had better go have your walk. You don't need to have puppy problems too."

"We sure don't need those." Priscilla stood up, and Jake leaped to his feet, panting eagerly. "I can't help wondering if it was a mistake to give Joan a dog. As a surprise, I mean. Maybe, as she says, she just really isn't ready."

"Do you think so? You know her much better than I do, of course, but it looked to me like she really loves Sister. How could you not?"

"She is precious, no doubt about it, but Joan still seems like she's not sure."

"They haven't been together very long yet," Kitty said. "Give them a little time. It's always a little rocky at first."

"Right."

Priscilla walked to the door, thinking. It was true. It took time to really develop a friendship. After so many years, Katherine Evans and Miss Waterman must have known just about everything about each other. Maybe it wasn't so crazy to think that Miss Waterman would bankrupt herself to keep her best friend safe.

"You know," she said, turning back to Kitty, "maybe we can find out more about that burglary when I get back. It can't be a coincidence that the museum just happened to get broken into right after Rowan Cavanaugh came into town."

Kitty shook her head. "If it is a coincidence, it's an awfully big one."

CHAPTER TEN

O fficer Brown," Priscilla said cheerfully when April picked up the phone. "This is Priscilla Grant. I was wondering if you have a few minutes to talk."

"Is this about your friend's aunt again?"

Priscilla cringed slightly and glanced over at Kitty, who sat on the couch next to her. April always got straight to the point. "Actually, I was wondering if you ever found out what happened at the Cavanaugh Museum. Were the stolen items ever found? Have you made any arrests?"

"We're still investigating," April said, "but so far it's a lot of nothing. Malcolm Waterman doesn't seem to think we'll find anything at all."

"He doesn't want you to check out Rowan Cavanaugh?"

"Why do you want to know about him in particular?" April asked warily. "Do you know something pertaining to the case?"

"Not really," Priscilla admitted. "I understand Malcolm told you Cavanaugh might be involved in the thefts, and I didn't know if you needed at least a little bit of corroboration."

April sighed. "Mrs. Grant," she said. "I am going to go against my better judgment this one time, and let you in on our investigation. Hopefully that will stop you from making wild conjectures with no evidence. The last thing we need is a private citizen running around making crazy accusations against a prominent elected official. Now, what is your 'little bit' of corroboration?"

Priscilla felt the sting, but regained her composure. "As I said, it's not much. It's just that Kitty and I heard him arguing with Malcolm the day before the robbery. It really was barely anything, but he wanted to buy everything in the museum that didn't belong to his family already, and Malcolm was digging his heels in about not selling."

"Actually," April said, hesitating, "Malcolm did mention that they might have been overheard, but when I pressed him about it, he was reluctant to name names."

"Why's that?"

"I don't know. He seems to have given up on recovering any of the stolen property. At any rate, the only person he's offered us as a possible suspect is very unlikely to have been involved."

"You've ruled out Rowan Cavanaugh?" Priscilla said, and Kitty's eyebrows went up.

"For now, at least," April admitted. "He says he's trying to keep his visit here as quiet as possible."

"Driving that black Lamborghini isn't exactly keeping things quiet."

"True, but he's in town alone. No chauffeur or personal assistants or anything like that. He claims he just wanted to relax for a few days and, when he heard the museum was shutting down, he went to see how much of his family's things he could get back."

"But why couldn't he have stolen what Malcolm wouldn't sell?" Priscilla asked. "He had people come and take away what already belonged to him. Why couldn't he have sent them back that night for the rest? Malcolm already had most of it boxed up."

"Not very likely," April said. "I know the guys Cavanaugh hired. There's no reason to think they'd be involved in something like that."

"Maybe Cavanaugh did it himself. You know, went to his hotel and made a big deal about going to his room for the night and then snuck out in the middle of the night."

April chuckled. "Not very likely. For one thing, he's in a bed-and-breakfast, very posh of course, and his room is right over the owner's. She swears she hears it every time someone comes down those stairs."

"So maybe she was asleep," Priscilla said.

Kitty tugged her arm and gave her a questioning look, but Priscilla only shook her head, wanting to wait until the conversation with April was over to explain.

"She says she would know," April said. "And if he did get by her, he still would have had to get his car out of the lot. She says it was full that night, and her son came in late and had to park in the drive leading to it. A couple of her guests were complaining first thing the next morning, because nobody could get in or out."

"But—"

"And where was he going to put boxes of museum artifacts in a little sports car like that?"

Priscilla frowned, thinking for a moment more. "Okay, suppose he snuck out and caught a cab."

"We checked those out too," April assured her. "Nobody went out to the inn that night, and again Cavanaugh would have had the problem of carrying off all those boxes. From what Malcolm said, it would be too much for a cab to hold."

"So he had his own people do it. From New York or wherever he lives these days. Don't tell me he couldn't arrange it."

April snorted. "No, I'm not going to tell you that. I'm more than sure that someone with his pull could arrange a job like this, but it seems highly unlikely in so short a period of time. Malcolm says Cavanaugh had never asked him about buying the museum displays before that day you heard them squabbling about it. He hadn't even met Cavanaugh before then."

"I thought the Cavanaughs and the Watermans were close."

"That was in Miss Waterman's day and before, from what I understand. Once the Cavanaughs really got into politics and jet-setting, once some of the older folks started dying off, they didn't stay in touch. To tell the truth, I don't remember Cavanaugh or any of his family showing up around here, not in Tisbury any-way, for a long time. Of course, they do have their mansion here."

Priscilla frowned. "Wait a minute. If he has a house here, why's he in a bed-and-breakfast?"

"I asked him that," April said. "He told me he was planning to be here for only a couple of days and didn't want to bother with opening up the house."

"I suppose that would be a hassle."

"DC or New York or LA is where they are most of the time, if not in Europe or someplace exotic. The Watermans are all over now too. Besides Malcolm and Miss Waterman herself, none of them still live on the island."

"Really? Where are they now?"

Kitty looked at Priscilla again, obviously dying to know what she and April were talking about. Priscilla held up one finger, urging her to be patient.

"All over, as I understand it," April said. "Married, moved on, I don't know. The story is that Miss Waterman wasn't very happy about that and wasn't happy they didn't stay in touch after they left. People say that's why she's such a recluse now."

Priscilla was more puzzled than ever. "What family does she have?"

"She had a brother who was killed in the Second World War, but he never married. She had another brother who was Malcolm's father. He's gone now, of course, and so is Malcolm's mother. I believe they had three or four other children, daughters, I think, who married and moved all over the mainland. Miss Waterman has a large number of nieces and nephews, and their children and grandchildren, who all ignore her equally."

Priscilla winced, thinking of how much she had missed out in her own family because of grudges and misunderstandings. "That's too bad. But what about Malcolm? He stayed in Tisbury. Why won't she see him?"

"I couldn't say. Probably something silly. In the grand scheme of things, that's usually what it boils down to. Money or pride or stubbornness—nothing that will be worth much when all's said and done."

"So you're telling me that Rowan Cavanaugh couldn't possibly have taken those things from the museum?"

"I'm not saying that at all," April said. "I'm just saying it seems very improbable at this point. He does have motive, but I'm not really seeing means or opportunity. There's just not enough there to pursue it, especially if Malcolm isn't willing to sign a complaint against him."

"He's not?" Priscilla gasped.

"He's not what?" Kitty whispered, and Priscilla waved at her to be quiet.

"He sounded like he was sure Cavanaugh was behind the theft," Priscilla protested.

"We told him we'd look into it," April said, "and when I asked him to clarify a few things a couple of days later, he said it wasn't any use fighting against people with that kind of pull, especially when he didn't have anything but conjecture about it in the first place. We can't force him to pursue it if he doesn't want to."

Priscilla didn't say anything for a minute, her thoughts racing. Should she tell April her concerns about that campaign ribbon being fake? Maybe it didn't matter too much now, not if everything in the museum was gone and Malcolm wasn't going to pursue finding the thief.

"I don't know," Priscilla admitted. "I just think Cavanaugh must have something to do with this. Did you know he came to see me and Kitty the other day? He was asking about her aunt and if her aunt ever told her anything about Rosie Cavanaugh or sent her anything that had to do with Rosie."

"That's not against the law," April reminded her.

"But he even knew that we had been at my cousin's house earlier. How could he have known that? It's creepy."

"I can understand that, but it's not something I can arrest him for."

"I know, but we can't figure out what he's after." Priscilla glanced over at Kitty and then plunged ahead. "When you saw Miss Waterman, how was she? Did she seem . . . competent?"

"I have to admit, I wasn't sure what I'd find up there. She's been a recluse for so long that there's kind of a mythos about her around here. But she was just a frail-looking lady. Besides being sort of startled to see me, she was fine. Perfectly competent and composed. A little withdrawn maybe, but I guess that's understandable after all this time. Maybe shy is a better word than withdrawn. There really wasn't anything remarkable about her. She seemed nice."

"That's good to know. She didn't happen to say anything about Katherine Evans, did she? I mean, more than what you already told us?"

"No," April said. "She told me about when Mrs. Evans died. That seemed to upset her some, but that's fairly normal. I got the feeling they were really good friends. Miss Waterman is pretty lonely, if you ask me."

"That doesn't surprise me at all. Anna Vaden doesn't seem the kind to sit up with her, watching old movies and playing cards. But that makes it all that much more strange that she refused to see Kitty, even for a minute, and doesn't want to keep writing to her. Kitty thought she would like having a pen pal."

Kitty nodded vigorously.

"She didn't happen to mention that she'd seen Cavanaugh, did she?" Priscilla asked.

"No," April said. "But I didn't ask her about him. Should I have?"

Priscilla sighed. "I don't know. I don't know how he fits in." Should she tell April about seeing Cavanaugh and Anna Vaden in Oak Bluffs? Maybe it wouldn't hurt. "He just seems really bent on finding out if Katherine Evans had anything of his grandmother's. It seems natural that, if she did, she would have had it with her at the Waterman house. Did you happen to talk to the housekeeper while you were there?"

"What does she have to do with anything?" April asked.

"We saw her when we were in Oak Bluffs."

"That's not particularly suspicious, you know."

"The thing is," Priscilla said, "we also saw Mr. Cavanaugh's Lamborghini. At least, I'm pretty sure it was his. How many could there be on the island?"

"Probably not that many."

"Anyway, we were thinking he and Anna must have met somewhere near the carousel, and the only reason we figure it could be is that they didn't want anyone to know about it. And that's what makes me wonder if Mr. Cavanaugh's been paying her off for some reason or if Miss Waterman has."

"Why would you think that?" April asked.

"She was driving a very nice car. Of course, that could be Miss Waterman's, but not the clothes and jewelry, I wouldn't think. Or if it is, that's something someone ought to look into."

"What exactly are you getting at?"

Priscilla gave Kitty a questioning look and got an encouraging nod in return.

"Okay, this might sound crazy. It probably is crazy, but we were wondering if maybe Katherine Evans might have known something about Rosie Cavanaugh because she worked for her before she worked for Miss Waterman. Or maybe she had something of Rosie's. We don't know. Whatever she had or knew, though, Mr. Cavanaugh seems to want to find out about it pretty badly."

"Okay." April's voice was calm and even, but Priscilla could tell she'd caught her interest at last. "And?"

"And, well, what if Katherine isn't dead at all?"

April cleared her throat, and Priscilla was sure it was to cover a laugh. "What makes you say that?"

"Okay, it's just a theory, but what if Katherine actually did know something about Rosie or about one of the family that Mr. Cavanaugh doesn't want getting out? Everybody around here says Katherine and Miss Waterman were great friends. Suppose Katherine realized that Mr. Cavanaugh was going to find out what she knew and would want to get rid of her to keep it quiet."

"Are you saying they faked Katherine Evans's death to protect her from Cavanaugh?"

Priscilla winced. "I guess it does sound pretty lame." She ignored Kitty's hurt expression. "We know it would be hard to pull off something like that, but suppose that's what they did. Now suppose the new housekeeper, Anna Vaden, found out about it and is blackmailing Miss Waterman. If Miss Waterman needs money, that would explain why she wants to sell her property."

"And the housekeeper's been living there for over two years and just now noticed that Miss Waterman is hiding someone in her attic?" April chuckled. "Okay."

"No. It looks to me like someone's been paying Anna off for a while now. If it's Miss Waterman, maybe she already used up the rest of her money and that's why she's selling now. Wouldn't that make sense?"

"Only if you buy the story about people faking deaths and blackmailing little old ladies."

Priscilla counted to ten. "I don't suppose Miss Waterman mentioned anything about the Cavanaughs when you were there," she finally said. "Anything at all?"

"No."

"And the housekeeper didn't either?"

"Why would either of them?" April sounded exasperated now. "That's not what I went there for. I didn't even know Cavanaugh was in town."

Priscilla bit her lip, thinking.

"Mrs. Grant, what is it you want me to do?" April asked her finally.

"Have you talked to Miss Waterman about the museum break-in? She's part owner of the things that were stolen."

"Malcolm's the one who called us in. Unless Miss Waterman wants us to continue the investigation, there's not much we can do about it."

"I was just wondering—" Priscilla looked over at Kitty. "*We* were just wondering if maybe you could go back out there and talk to her. Ask her about the break-in and if she wants to pursue the matter."

"That's not the way we usually handle things," April said.

"But then you could have another look around the place. You could, while you're talking about the break-in, tell her Mr. Cavanaugh was asking to buy the things from the museum and that he had come to talk to Kitty about what her aunt might have had of his grandmother's. Maybe ask her if he came to see her. Or asked to see her."

"Mrs. Grant—"

"Or ask the housekeeper if he was there. No, she probably wouldn't tell you if he came to talk to her. Not if they're in cahoots."

"Look, we can't just go around bothering people without a reason. If Cavanaugh did something illegal, and I don't think that's very probable, at least in this instance, then it seems like it's been settled to Malcolm's satisfaction."

"But if that's the case, if Malcolm was paid off, then hasn't Miss Waterman still been defrauded? That stuff was hers too."

April exhaled. "Okay, I'll go see her again. I'll tell her about the break-in, just in case she doesn't already know about it, and I'll ask her about Cavanaugh. And I'll ask the housekeeper if she's talked to Cavanaugh. I can usually tell if someone's not straight with me."

"And could you—"

"I'll keep my eyes open to see if there's any sign of anyone but the two of them living there. That's the best I can do short of accusing them of having faked Mrs. Evans's death and demanding to be shown through the house. I'd need a lot more to go on and a search warrant before that's going to happen."

Priscilla smiled at Kitty. "Thank you, April. I think Kitty and I would both feel better if you could at least talk to Miss Waterman one more time."

"I'm making no promises," April warned her. "But I'll see if I can turn up anything. Meanwhile, you both stay out of trouble. If you think something illegal is going on, you'd better report it to us and let us handle it. That's what we get paid for, and you two don't need to be getting into something over your heads."

"We'll be careful," Priscilla assured her. "But we appreciate your finding out as much as you can."

"Okay. But keep quiet about this. I'll never live it down if the rest of the department finds out I'm trying to raise the dead. You take care."

"Tell me what she said," Kitty demanded the instant Priscilla put down her phone. "Hearing just one side was driving me crazy."

Priscilla filled her in. "It doesn't sound like there's much more she can do unless we actually find out about something criminal."

"Well, there's something weird about that museum stuff. Why did Malcolm want to keep it so badly and now suddenly doesn't care? And who would want it besides him and Mr. Cavanaugh?"

Kitty thought for a second. "I guess there are a lot of memorabilia collectors out there."

"Right," Priscilla said. "We just have to keep our eyes open and see what we see."

"Well, we'd better do it soon," Kitty told her. "I have to go home eventually. My boss is understanding, but that's going to run out before too much longer."

"I think you should stay and help me with the lighthouse museum until April gets a chance to go back to see Miss Waterman. After that, maybe it's time we give up."

Kitty sighed. Giving up was something neither of them really wanted to do.

CHAPTER ELEVEN

Priscilla and Kitty spent the rest of the afternoon working on an exhibit about the building of the lighthouse in 1852.

"That's just perfect," Priscilla said after Kitty had arranged the original plans of the lighthouse, information about its being moved twice due to soil erosion, and some mid-nineteenth-century tools that had been up in the attic into a logical and pleasing display. "I can never repay you for helping me so much on this."

"And I can never repay you for letting me stay with you while I'm here and for helping me find out more about what happened with my aunt."

"Sounds like we must be even, then," Priscilla said with a smile. "Now, what do you think? I've been considering painting in here. The paint's not bad as it is, but I'd like to freshen it up for the grand opening—if I ever get everything done so I can have a grand opening." She rummaged in her pocket and took out some paint chips, varieties of off-white and cream, some light tans, some soft yellows. "I want to keep the historical look and feel, of course, so I don't want to go with any really strong colors or anything stark."

They discussed the paint chips for a few minutes. Gardenia was too orangey, Ice Cube was too gray, and Glimmer was too green. China Doll was a lovely shade of tan, but Priscilla was afraid it might be too dark and make the room look small. Casa Blanca was a lighter version of China Doll, and very pretty too. Kitty campaigned for that one, but Priscilla made her admit she only wanted it because she liked the movie. They finally agreed on Roman Column, a slightly-yellowed off-white.

"That will cheer up everything," Kitty said.

Priscilla squinted, trying to imagine the room freshly painted, and nodded. "I think so. It's not an actual yellow, just enough to warm up the white."

She put a checkmark next to Roman Column and then turned to pick up the eighteenth-century sextant she had found up in the attic. "This," she told Kitty, "is our next exhibit."

"Ooh." Kitty's eyes lit up. "That's fabulous. What is it?"

"It's a sextant. Navigators on ships used them to chart their courses based on the stars. This one is way older than the lighthouse. I'm thinking one of the seafaring Lathams must have owned it, but I don't have any information about that. I just thought it would be interesting to display it and show how it works."

"Do you know how it works?" Kitty asked, one eyebrow raised.

Priscilla sighed. "Not in the least, and everything I got off the Internet that's supposed to explain it just makes me more confused. Something about reflected angles and celestial bodies and I don't know what."

"I bet your Coast Guard friend would love to explain it to you," Kitty said, a gleam of mischief in her eyes.

"I hate to spoil your fun, but I think you're absolutely right. He ought to be able to explain it in layman's terms so I can write up something for the display. Good idea."

"Spoilsport," Kitty said, pouting, and then she smiled. "He seems like a nice guy."

"He is, and he's always here to help if something goes wrong with the lighthouse, since the Coast Guard operates it."

"Ooh." Kitty pursed her lips. "Cozy, isn't it?"

"Oh, hush," Priscilla said, laughing. "We're just—"

A brisk knock cut her off. She glanced questioningly at Kitty and then went to open the lighthouse door. Malcolm Waterman stood there, glaring at her from behind his thick glasses.

Priscilla stared back. "I, uh, wasn't expecting anyone. Is there something I can do for you?"

"Why do you have to go around stirring things up?" he demanded, storming into the lighthouse. "Aren't things messed up enough as it is?"

"I'm sure I don't—"

"The museum's gone now. Why can't you let it go?" He looked around, obviously unimpressed with her own exhibits. "I guess you wouldn't want any competition. Not if this is all you've got."

"It's not done yet," Kitty said with a pugnacious thrust of her chin.

Malcolm huffed.

"What exactly are we supposed to have done?" Priscilla asked.

"Stirring up the police again," he snapped. "Don't tell me that wasn't you, because they all but told me it was. They said 'someone' told them about the conversation I had with Cavanaugh, that day you two were eavesdropping. Well, there wasn't anything in that at all, so you don't have any business saying there was."

"I was trying to help you find out who robbed your museum," Priscilla protested. "You practically told me Cavanaugh was the one behind it. How was I supposed to know you changed your mind all of a sudden?"

"I didn't change my mind. I just didn't have much to go on, and once I thought about it calmly, I decided I didn't have enough evidence to really pursue the idea. You should have kept out of it."

"I was surprised to hear you had decided not to have the police follow up on the case. How could I have known?"

He pressed his lips into a tight line, glaring at her. "Well, now you do know, so back off. Don't I have enough to worry about with all the rest of the family being on my case?"

Priscilla's eyebrows went up. "I didn't know they were."

"Well, they are, so I can do without busybodies making things worse."

"Forgive me for trying to be helpful," Priscilla said coolly.

"All right, fine." Malcolm exhaled. "I just have enough to deal with without people here making things more difficult. How am I supposed to know what Aunt Caroline is going to do or why she wants to sell that land? I told them to contact her lawyer. That's what I have to do, and I live less than two miles from her."

Priscilla glanced at Kitty and then back at Malcolm. "Who's 'them'?"

"Oh, my sisters," he grumbled. "They haven't bothered to keep in touch for years, but now that their 'inheritance' might be sold off, they jump right on it."

"What did the lawyer tell them?"

He sneered. "Only that he had passed on their concerns and would contact them if and when Aunt Caroline had anything to tell them."

"Why don't they keep in touch with her themselves?" Priscilla asked.

"Why doesn't your aunt talk to you?" Kitty added. "You didn't move away."

"My sisters," he said disdainfully, "got married and moved off. I don't know why she doesn't keep in touch with them, and I don't care. I would have cut them off altogether, if I were her. In her will, I mean. I don't know. Maybe she has by now." He snorted. "Maybe she's cut out all of us, crazy old bat."

Priscilla and Kitty both looked at him coldly.

Finally he shrugged. "I never hear a word from any of my sisters unless they find out Aunt Caroline is doing something they don't like. 'Oh, Malcolm,'" he said, imitating a female voice, "'what's she doing now? Can't you get her to stop? Why don't you go see her and tell her how silly she's being.' As if I could!"

"You've spoken to them recently?" Priscilla asked.

"They've spoken to me. Or I should say, they've ordered me around as usual. They even threatened to come out here and talk to her, but I told them she won't see them, so there's no use wasting a lot of money and time just to bash their heads against a very stubborn brick wall." He shook his head. "Then they act like I'm trying to hide something from them or make Aunt Caroline do something besides just what she wants to do. Humph. I should have told them to come on out. Would have served them right. Besides, why should she see them when she won't even see me?"

"Why won't she see you?" Priscilla asked again, making the question sound as casual as possible. "You stayed on the island. You took over the museum after your father died, right? Shouldn't that have made her happy?"

"Well, it didn't, okay?" he snapped.

"But I don't understand," Kitty said. "Why wouldn't she—"

"Look, what happened between us is my business. It has nothing to do with the break-in, and certainly nothing to do with either of you."

"Okay," Kitty said after a moment's pause. "Sorry."

Priscilla tilted her head to one side. "I'm still wondering what happened to the things that were stolen from your museum. If you don't think it was Cavanaugh, who do you think it was?"

He shrugged his hunched shoulders. "I don't know. The stuff wasn't worth that much, and there's not a lot I can do about it now. I'll just have to move on."

"What are you going to do?" Kitty asked, a touch of sympathy in her expression.

"I'm not sure yet. There's some insurance money coming. Half of it, anyway. The other half is Aunt Caroline's. She's not likely to keep my checks coming now that there isn't a museum for me to run."

"I thought you had wanted her to close it," Priscilla said.

"Yeah, years ago. When I thought I'd be some kind of photo-journalist and win a Pulitzer Prize or something. Then I got older and pretty comfortable where I was, and traveling around the world with nothing but a knapsack didn't sound so attractive anymore."

"Things change as time goes by." Priscilla hesitated a moment. "I have to ask you about something I noticed last time I was in your museum. I mean, the last time before the break-in."

He looked at her expectantly.

"Well," Priscilla said, "I just happened to notice that one of those World War II campaign ribbons didn't look authentic. Are you sure you didn't get fleeced by whoever might have sold them to you?"

He drew himself up to his full five-foot-eight. "Those ribbons were given to my father by Rowan Cavanaugh II for inclusion in our collection. I suppose he'd know whether they were authentic or not. Actually, that part of the collection belonged to my father entirely, so they were passed down to me. Aunt Caroline didn't own any portion of them."

"I suppose it doesn't matter now, if they're gone anyway," Priscilla said. "I just wonder what a thief would want with something like that." She eyed him speculatively. "I suppose if a real collector wanted something badly enough, he wouldn't ask too many questions."

"I hope," he said, his tone frigid, "you aren't implying that anyone in my family would have bought stolen goods to put into the collection."

She held up both hands. "No, no. Not at all. That never entered my mind."

"Well, it shouldn't." Malcolm was suddenly sulky. "If we had bought something that had been stolen and put it on display, it would be found out pretty quickly. I'm not quite that stupid."

"I suppose," Priscilla said, "a lot of collectors don't care about displaying their collections. Not like a museum or anything. They just like building their collections and enjoying them in private. They say a lot of the famous art that has been stolen over the years is probably in private collections."

Malcolm shrugged. "I suppose. I wouldn't know about that in particular."

"No. I suppose not."

"I just came to find out if you were through meddling in my business."

Priscilla felt a pull of conscience. "I didn't mean to cause you any trouble."

"I suppose not. Anyway, I'll let you get back to your work. I hope you have better luck than I did with the museum."

Priscilla stopped him when he reached the door. "I was wondering, though, when you planned to close your exhibit."

Malcolm turned warily. "I had expected it to happen any time over the past few weeks. Why do you ask?"

"It's just that you didn't mention it when I first came to visit."

"Of course I did. I told you to have a look, because it might not be open too much longer."

"But you didn't make it sound like it was going to close in the next day or two," Priscilla said.

Kitty nodded. "You didn't say anything when I was there, and the museum was robbed that same night."

Malcolm shrugged. "How was I supposed to know that?"

"But you had everything packed up before the burglary," Priscilla said. "Or did I hear the story wrong?"

He pressed his lips together. "No."

"Did your aunt contact you and tell you to close up?"

"No." He glared at them both. "If you must know, after Cavanaugh and I had our little discussion that day, I decided I was going to go ahead and call it quits. I was the one running the place. Aunt Caroline couldn't possibly care if it closed up a day or a week or a month earlier than she would have closed it in the first place. To be honest, I was afraid Cavanaugh might have something up his sleeve once he picked up everything that belonged to his family. I just figured I'd pack it all up and get it out of there."

"But what were you going to do with it?" Kitty asked. "If your aunt sells the house the museum was in, where were you going to put the exhibits?"

"I don't know." Malcolm sighed. "Maybe I'd have opened up somewhere else. Everything happened so fast. I just wasn't going to let Cavanaugh bully me out of it."

Priscilla smiled. "At least you'll have a bit of insurance money to help you get started again."

"It's not much," he told her, but he didn't say any more.

It would be interesting to know how much was not much.

CHAPTER TWELVE

Y ou think he took those things himself, don't you?" Kitty asked. "For the insurance money?"

"It's possible." Priscilla watched through the lighthouse window until Malcolm drove away. "But I'm not sure it makes sense. If he was in it for the money, why not take Cavanaugh's offer? Whatever he wants so badly, it sounded like he was willing to pay. I can't imagine Malcolm's half of the insurance money would be better than what Cavanaugh would have given him."

"It doesn't seem very likely." Kitty sighed. "Well, at least the police must have asked him a few more questions. Do you think your friend April has gone to see Miss Waterman yet?"

"I don't think so. I suppose it's possible, but I think she'd call and tell us how it went if she had already."

"Yeah, I suppose."

They worked on the next exhibit in silence for a few minutes longer. Then there was another knock on the door.

Kitty's eyes widened. "You don't think...?"

"I can't imagine it's Malcolm again," Priscilla said. "But I don't know who else it would be."

She opened the door and let out a relieved breath. "Gerald. How are you? Come in."

"Hey." He gave her a hint of a smile and swept off his hat. "Sorry to just drop in, but I wanted to make sure you both were okay. Hey, Kitty."

Kitty beamed at him. "Hi."

"You're always welcome," Priscilla said. "But why wouldn't we be okay?"

He shrugged. "I was just patrolling, and I saw Malcolm Waterman's car up here. I know you've been interested in the museum. So I thought I'd just check."

Kitty looked smug. "I told you there was nothing wrong with having a handsome sailor looking after you."

Priscilla gave her a stern look, and Gerald chuckled.

"We're fine," Priscilla said. "Still wondering about those things that were stolen."

"I think Malcolm is behind it himself somehow," Kitty put in. "I just don't know why, if it's not for the insurance."

Gerald frowned. "Now I'm starting to wonder. I saw his car out on one of the piers last night. I wasn't sure it was his at first, but I saw it pull to the end of the pier, and then the headlights went out. I just sat back and watched. Of course I couldn't see much, and then the lights came back on and the car started backing toward the road again. I pulled my boat up closer and saw that it was Malcolm's car, but a few seconds later, he was gone."

"What do you think he was doing?" Priscilla asked.

"Hard to say. If I was guessing, I'd say getting rid of something. The ocean is pretty good for that in general, though he'd have done better to get farther away from shore."

"I suppose it could be the items that were taken from the museum," Kitty said. "But why? If he didn't want them, why didn't he just sell them to Mr. Cavanaugh?"

"Maybe because they're fakes," Priscilla said.

"And he didn't want Mr. Cavanaugh to know they were fakes." Kitty thought for a second. "He couldn't sell them to anyone because they were fakes, but why were they fakes in the first place? What happened to the real things?"

"Wait a minute," Gerald said. "Are you saying not everything in the Cavanaugh Museum was authentic?"

"I don't know for sure," Priscilla admitted, "but I noticed one of the campaign ribbons looked wrong, just based on something someone told me a few years ago. Before I could do any research about it or look around any more, the museum was broken into and everything was gone."

Gerald's eyes narrowed. "And Malcolm doesn't want the police to keep investigating? Sounds like he realized he'd gotten in a little too deep and decided to get rid of the evidence."

Priscilla nodded. "I think he took advantage of Cavanaugh's visit to stage the break-in. Of course Cavanaugh would be an obvious suspect after their 'discussion' that day. But then maybe Malcolm got cold feet and thought he'd better just let the thing drop, especially considering that it *is* Cavanaugh. I understand there's insurance involved too. I can't imagine they wouldn't investigate to see if he was involved. Insurance fraud, filing a false police report, false accusation, I don't know what all—but it wouldn't look good for him to be found with the supposedly stolen property after that."

"I still want to know what happened to the real items," Kitty said. "Why were there fakes in the museum in the first place?"

"You heard what I said to Malcolm," Priscilla told her. "There are collectors who'll buy things with no questions asked. They don't want to display them to the public. They just want to have them. I don't know this for sure, but I'd say he found someone, or several someones, he could sell the things to. Maybe he even did it over several years' time. It could have just been a few things here or there, things he could replace with good replicas that most people wouldn't notice. Who really looks in detail at museum exhibits? Sure, there would be some experts who would realize there were fakes in with the authentic items, but most people just look and read the stories about the items. That's what they go for."

"You noticed," Gerald said.

"I just happened to notice." Priscilla shook her head. "I'm no expert, but I had heard something before about those campaign ribbons. I guess I'm just naturally inquisitive."

He gave her a conspiratorial smile that made all this fuss about Malcolm Waterman worthwhile. "So Malcolm panicked and dumped the stuff in the ocean."

"Wouldn't that be a lot of things to throw into the water?" Kitty asked. "Wouldn't it wash up?"

"That would depend on how well it was packed up and weighed down. How much stuff do you think there was?"

Priscilla pursed her lips. "I don't know. Could be a lot. I don't know how many of the items in the museum belonged to Malcolm and Miss Waterman, and how many of them were on loan. Malcolm talked about having boxes of things, but I'm assuming he meant big boxes. Maybe it's not all that much after all. I don't really have much to go on."

"Could somebody go down there and look?" Kitty asked. "A diver?"

Gerald shrugged. "They could, but unless Malcolm's breaking a federal law, there's nothing I can do about it officially. It would be best to just tell the police what you suspect and let them take it from there. Even if he did dispose of the stuff, it was his in the first place. Unless you want him picked up for polluting the ocean."

Priscilla shook her head. "There is the question of insurance money he shouldn't get and Miss Waterman's half of whatever jointly owned items he might have sold. But maybe we can use what we know to get him to tell us more than he seems willing to say right now."

"You think we ought to go talk to him now?" Kitty asked, and she sounded a little breathless.

"I mean exactly that. He didn't mind dropping in on us. It would only be neighborly to return the call." Priscilla looked at Gerald. "I suppose your boat's tied up at my dock."

He nodded.

"Would you mind coming along with us? If Malcolm knows you saw him last night, he might be willing to tell us everything."

"I'd be happy to. If I don't tell him it isn't an official Coast Guard call right away, it ought to make him a little more cooperative."

Priscilla looked around the room. There were open boxes and a number of lighthouse-related family heirlooms lying around in no particular order. "I think everything will be fine the way it is for a few minutes, don't you, Kitty?"

Kitty looked unsure for a moment, and then she grinned. "All right, I'm game. I don't know what I'm doing, acting like I'm a detective or something, but I'm not about to be left out."

They got into Priscilla's SUV, and once they were all buckled up, Priscilla started to laugh. "I just realized I don't have a clue where he lives."

"Amateur," Gerald said with a grin, and he got out his phone. Less than a minute later, he had an address and directions to a cottage just a short distance away. "This is it," he said when they pulled up in front. "And that's definitely the car I saw last night."

Malcolm Waterman's green Acura was big enough to carry a reasonable amount of cargo.

Priscilla stared at the cottage for a moment and then turned off the engine. "Ready?"

It was a minute or two before Malcolm opened the door, scowling when he saw them. "I didn't think—" He noticed Gerald. "Who're you?"

Gerald smiled and thrust out his hand. "I'm Gerald O'Bannon. I'm with the Coast Guard."

Malcolm turned more pale than usual. "Look, I don't know what these two told you, but I really think I've been harassed enough. Is this an official visit?"

Gerald still smiled. "Do you want it to be?"

Malcolm gaped at him.

"Look," Gerald said, "all we want to do is come in for a minute or two and have a talk. It doesn't have to be anything major. To be honest, I'm just here as a friend of these ladies. Whether or not it gets to be more than that is up to you."

Malcolm stepped back to let them inside. The cottage was neither large nor luxurious, but it was cozy enough, decently if unimaginatively furnished. The large flat-screen television was paused on an action-adventure movie. A glass of what looked like some variety of cola was on the end table next to the easy chair.

Malcolm turned off the TV. "Okay, so talk."

Priscilla looked at Kitty and Gerald and then decided to jump right in. "We'd like to know why you dumped the counterfeits you had in your museum."

As she had hoped, he looked shaken by her certainty. For a minute she thought he was going to rally and deny the whole thing, but he only sank into his chair, head in his hands.

"How did you know?"

"That campaign ribbon I was looking at. The pin was wrong."

Malcolm shook his head, mouth hard. "I knew it. I knew I should have fixed that. Nobody would have noticed if the stupid thing hadn't fallen over. I knew you'd seen it, but I didn't think anybody would know the difference."

"So you really *were* behind the break-in?" Kitty asked. "You stole all your own museum exhibits?"

"And then you dumped all your fakes off the pier last night," Gerald said conversationally.

Malcolm looked at him for a moment. "You saw me, I guess."

Gerald nodded.

"I guess I'm pretty miserable at this sort of thing." Malcolm sighed. "So what now? Are you headed over to tell the police? Of course you are. What am I supposed to do, congratulate you?"

"Maybe the police don't have to come into it at all," Priscilla suggested.

Malcolm snorted. "You could have fooled me."

"Look," Gerald said, "could we all sit down? Let's not make this any more uncomfortable than we have to."

Malcolm swept his arms out wide, indicating the couch and the other chair. "Knock yourselves out."

Kitty took the chair at the opposite end of the couch from Malcolm's recliner. Gerald and Priscilla sat on the couch with Priscilla next to Malcolm.

"We're not trying to get anyone in trouble," she began. "We're just trying to figure out what's going on here and what this situation with Cavanaugh and your museum has to do with Kitty's aunt."

Malcolm frowned. "Her aunt? How should I know?"

"What in particular was Cavanaugh after?"

"He didn't really say," Malcolm admitted. "He asked me about books and letters, and when I told him I didn't know what he was talking about, that I didn't have anything to do with his grandmother, he said he wanted to buy everything I had that wasn't his already. As you well know, I could hardly do that. If anyone would spot a fake, it would be Cavanaugh." He looked suddenly wistful. "And he was offering a pretty nice price too."

"So he was asking specifically about his grandmother," Priscilla said. "Did he say why?"

Malcolm shook his head. "I suppose he thought if I knew what he really wanted, the price would go up."

"How long have you been selling off things from the museum?" Gerald asked, looking Malcolm over as if he were an unexpected variety of fish that had turned up in his net.

"Oh, maybe four or five years now. I found a collector advertising online for political memorabilia, and I got in touch. He didn't much mind how I came by the items as long as he could buy them from me. It was just a few petty things at first—some autographed photos, some medals, nothing worth much. Just enough to catch up on some bills and things, you know? But over time, I started selling off some of the rarer items, some of the guns and jewelry, those sorts of things."

"Was there really that much money in it?" Kitty asked him.

"I was surprised, to tell the truth. I mean, not so much I could retire or anything like that, but a few hundred here and there, sometimes more depending on the particular item. It wasn't bad. Not bad at all. As long as people are fascinated by the Cavanaughs, I guess there's going to be a market."

That was true. It had been Cavanaugh's grandfather, Rowan Cavanaugh II, who had really been the darling of the post-war media. War hero, married to an ethereally beautiful, gracious lady who seemed always poised, always stylish. Their pictures had been in all the newspapers and magazines, they spoke on radio programs, were featured in newsreels, and later on, appeared on fledgling television broadcasts, their every move followed by an adoring public.

Rosie Cavanaugh's sudden death from liver cancer at the age of only forty-seven had shocked the nation and the world. Her husband had married twice after that, once at fifty and once at seventy-three, but no one seemed to consider those marriages of any consequence. He was forever linked to Rosie, icon of an era, the tragic beauty who never grew old.

"I suppose the current Cavanaugh is about the last of them," Priscilla considered. "The rest of the family doesn't seem much interested in politics or world affairs."

Malcolm shrugged. "I wouldn't know about that. They seem much like my own family now, scattered all over, too busy to keep in touch. Not like it was sixty or seventy years ago when they stuck together, back when even the Watermans and the Cavanaughs were close. It's all gone. Now we don't even talk."

They were all silent for a moment.

"Why did your aunt stop talking to you?" Priscilla asked finally.

He shot her a hard look and then shrugged. "All right, if you want to know, some years ago I met a girl I really liked. I, uh—" He cleared his throat. "I haven't had a lot of luck with women in my life, and I had about given up on ever finding someone."

Priscilla didn't say anything, but she couldn't help imagining him collecting action figures. Not that there weren't women out there who found that appealing.

"Anyway," he continued, "this girl, Janice, came into the museum one day, and we started talking. I eventually asked her out, and things went great for a few months. I even thought about asking her to marry me. Then all of a sudden she said she was done. She said it had been fun, but she was tired of me and she was leaving."

"Oh," Kitty breathed.

Priscilla shook her head. "That's too bad."

"That's not the kicker, though," he said with a wry twist of his mouth. "I knew Aunt Caroline hadn't liked Janice from the first. She told me I ought to look out for fortune hunters because of the money she was eventually going to leave me. I thought that was pretty ridiculous at the time, but then I found out why Janice broke off our relationship."

Kitty looked at him expectantly. Almost afraid she already knew what he was going to say, so did Priscilla.

He huffed. "She offered Janice money to leave the island, and Janice took it." His laugh was soft and bitter. "She took it."

CHAPTER THIRTEEN

B ut why should that make your aunt refuse to speak to you?"
Priscilla asked Malcolm when no one else said anything. "She
had to have known you would be upset to lose the woman you
loved so much."

Malcolm had the grace to look ashamed. "I didn't handle it
very well when I found out." He looked up at the ceiling and
shook his head. "I don't know why I'm telling you this. It sounds
pretty lame now. Anyway, I really lit into Aunt Caroline over it. I
told her to stay out of my life. I told her I was done with her except
for business matters."

"But she was just trying to help," Kitty said. "It looks like this
girl of yours really was in it for the money." She blinked at the glare
Malcolm shot her. "I mean, she, um…" She blinked again and
didn't say anything else.

"Yes." Malcolm's voice was sarcastically sweet. "Yes, Janice was
in it for the money. Yes, Aunt Caroline saved me from being taken
in by her. And after I'd cooled off, I wanted to tell my aunt I realized what she'd done and that she was trying to protect me, but by
then she had decided she wasn't going to see anyone anymore.
Ever. Even before that, she had stopped trying to stay in touch
with my sisters and their families, so what was one more? It's not

like I ever actually spent time with her anyway. So that's all there is to it."

"That's sad," Kitty said, and it was obvious she meant it. She'd always had a tender heart.

"And you've never tried to get back in touch with her?" Priscilla asked.

Malcolm made a sour face. "Once. A couple of years ago. I'm not getting any younger, and I was thinking about who I have in the world. There's not many. So I thought I'd try to smooth things over with the family. I sent each of my sisters a letter. One of them wrote back saying I'd have to come visit sometime but not quite yet because she's really busy. One texted me to say she got my note, and it was nice to hear from me. The other didn't answer at all."

"Ouch," Priscilla whispered.

"Then I wrote to Aunt Caroline. I apologized for what I had said the last time we spoke and for not trying to stay in touch, and I asked if we could possibly have a talk. What I got in response was a letter from her attorney saying that she would prefer I address any concerns regarding her directly to him. That was all." Malcolm exhaled. "I guess that was a lot more than you wanted to hear."

"I don't know what to say," Priscilla admitted. "It's not easy to keep relationships going. I'm sorry."

"Yeah, well, all that to say, I'd appreciate you both staying out of my business from now on."

"There's still this museum business," Gerald reminded him, his expression stern.

Malcolm ducked his head and shifted in his chair.

"You're very, very sure," Priscilla said, "that you didn't have anything about Katherine Evans in your collection? Not a mention in a letter or a diary or anything?"

"No. There just isn't anything." Malcolm glanced at Kitty. "I remember your aunt, but only from Aunt Caroline's house. The stuff with the Cavanaughs was well before my time."

"None of those photographs in the museum were of Katherine Evans?" Priscilla pressed. "Not with Rosie Cavanaugh or anything?"

"No," Malcolm said. "I knew the date and occasion of every picture we had on display and every person that was in them. I would have known if Katherine was there, even if most of those photos were only copies now anyway." He drew his thick brows together. "What difference would it make if she was?"

"I don't know. Maybe it would be a clue to what Cavanaugh is looking for and why he was asking Kitty about her."

"So those picture copies were part of what you dumped in the ocean," Gerald said.

Malcolm looked wary. "Yeah."

"What else?"

"Everything." Malcolm sighed. "All the fakes that had been on display. I couldn't let anybody find them."

"What about the genuine things?" Priscilla asked.

"I..." He squirmed. "I put them up in my attic."

Kitty gaped at him.

Gerald's expression did not change. "In your attic? You didn't think that's one of the first places the police might look if they suspect what you have done?"

"I packed everything in different boxes. Under layers of books or in with the Christmas decorations, that sort of thing. I couldn't very well throw away valuable collectibles like that."

"I see. And when the insurance adjuster comes to question you about the so-called theft?"

Malcolm cleared his throat. "I, uh, I told the insurance people I wasn't going to make a claim after all. Look, I didn't want to get into anything with them, just like I didn't want to get into anything with Cavanaugh and the police. I took the stuff, and I dumped most of it. I kept the rest." He squared his shoulders and thrust out his chin. "If you're going to turn me in, then do it. Cavanaugh already got back everything his family loaned the museum. As far as I can tell, I owe Aunt Caroline half of what I got for the stuff I sold and half of what I still have. Otherwise, nobody's out a penny."

Priscilla glanced over at Gerald. Malcolm was right, even if his intentions had been worse than what he had actually dared to carry out.

Gerald's face was unreadable. "So let me get this straight," he said to Malcolm. "You know nothing about what Cavanaugh's after, and you have no information about Katherine Evans that would have any connection with Cavanaugh or his family, right?"

Malcolm nodded.

Gerald's expression turned hard. "You realize if I ever find out you're not telling me the truth, I'll make sure you're sorry for it."

Again Malcolm nodded. "I've told you all I know. Whatever Cavanaugh wants, he didn't tell me."

"How many boxes of stuff did you throw into the ocean?" Gerald asked.

"Uh, four, I think. Yeah, four."

"Okay," Gerald said after a moment's thought. "Here's what you do. You hire a diver to go out there and dredge up all the trash you threw off the pier, and I mean all of it. When you have it, you give me a call. I want to see it. After that, you'd better never get caught at something like this again, got it?"

Malcolm looked as if he might protest, but then he merely exhaled. "Got it."

"And if I happen to go diving around there in the next week or two, I had better not see that there's any of it left."

"Yeah, yeah. I got it."

"Okay." Gerald's stern expression didn't relax, but Priscilla could tell he was satisfied all the same. "Is there anything else you ought to tell me? Anything I'm going to come after you about if I find out about it later on?"

"I swear, that's all I know."

"I want to ask about one more thing," Priscilla said. "Before we go."

Malcolm looked at her expectantly.

"You said you sent your aunt a letter saying you wanted to reconcile."

"Right."

"And that was when?" Priscilla asked.

"Two years ago, more or less."

"Can you narrow it down for me? At least the month?"

Malcolm bit his lip, thinking. "It must have been around Christmas. I just remember feeling pretty cut off from everybody and wanting to get back in touch." There was a sudden wryness in his expression. "For all the good it did me."

"And she never got in touch with you afterward? About anything?"

"Nothing," Malcolm admitted. "Not even from her lawyer. I got my checks for running the museum, but those were deposited automatically. That was it. I didn't try again."

"This is none of my business," Priscilla admitted, "but I'm curious. You say your aunt paid you to run the museum. It didn't make money itself?"

He laughed half under his breath. "Well, she and my father bought the old Cavanaugh house a long while back, as I told you before, to put the exhibits in. They thought it was a piece of history that shouldn't be lost. We don't charge admission, and what we make off the few books and photograph reprints we sell doesn't even pay the light bill. So yeah, she gives me a salary. Not a bad one, either, if you don't mind sitting around being bored most of the day and telling the same Cavanaugh stories over and over again."

"Thank you." Priscilla stood up, and Kitty and Gerald followed suit.

Malcolm got up too, and Kitty touched his arm.

"Maybe you should try again," she said gently. "I think she must be lonely up there, poor thing. I don't know if that housekeeper of hers is much company, really."

For a moment his expression was soft and vulnerable, and then that wryness covered it. "Her choice, isn't it?"

Kitty had no answer for that.

"I suppose you'll settle with her for what you took," Gerald said in a tone that was more of a directive than a conjecture.

Malcolm gritted his teeth. "I'll get in touch with her lawyer about it."

"See that you do. And I expect to hear from you about that recovery operation."

Malcolm made an overly formal bow in response and let them out.

"Do you do a lot of diving?" Kitty asked Gerald as Priscilla drove them back to the cottage.

"No." Gerald grinned at her. "But he doesn't have to know that."

Kitty giggled and then looked at Priscilla. "What's wrong?"

"Oh, nothing," Priscilla said with a belated smile. "I was just pondering what he said about trying to reconcile with his aunt around Christmas two years ago."

Kitty looked puzzled.

"Christmas two years ago would have been not very long after your aunt Katherine died. If she was upset about her nieces moving away and not staying in touch, it just seems odd to me that, when her only relation here on the island tries to reconcile with her, she refuses. I don't know what that has to do with your aunt's death, if anything. It just makes me wonder."

"What do you mean?" Kitty's eyes widened. "Oh. Oh, what if Aunt Katherine *is* still alive and hiding at Miss Waterman's? Miss Waterman couldn't let Malcolm come visit after that, could she?"

Gerald leaned up into the space between the two front seats to gape at her. "Wait. What? What are you two talking about?"

Priscilla grinned sheepishly. "I know it sounds crazy. It's just something we've been wondering about. We thought maybe Kitty's aunt didn't die and was hiding from Cavanaugh. Because of whatever it is he's looking for about his grandmother."

Kitty turned a little pink. "It was mostly something I was wondering about. I'm not even sure I think it's true, but then sometimes I do. I wish I still had some of Aunt Katherine's letters from the past couple of years. I could get the handwriting compared to one of her older ones or something. That would show for sure if she had written the last ones, wouldn't it?"

"You didn't keep any of the recent ones?" Gerald asked.

"No. I'm sure I didn't. I kept a couple of Christmas and birthday cards because I thought they were pretty, and a card she sent when Keith and I got married, but that's all. They're decades old."

"April Brown is looking into all this for us," Priscilla told Gerald. "She doesn't have anything that would let her get a search warrant, of course, but she said she'd go back out to the house and ask a few questions when she got a chance. Maybe she can tell us more after that."

"*Back* to the house?" Gerald asked.

"Well, we did have her go out once already, just to see if Miss Waterman was all right," Kitty admitted. "And then Priscilla convinced her to go back again, just to see if she noticed anything that would indicate there's someone living there besides Miss Waterman and the housekeeper."

"We haven't heard back from her yet. Maybe she didn't find anything. Or maybe—"

Her phone rang, not any of the special ringtones for her friends and family, and she smiled at Kitty. "Maybe that's her." She looked at the display. It was April. Priscilla pulled over and answered. "Hey. We were just wondering whether you'd found out anything new."

"I found out enough to convince me that nothing crazy is going on at that house. Miss Waterman agreed to see me again, and we had a pleasant little chat. She did know about the break-in. She said her nephew had informed her attorney about it, but she didn't seem at all concerned about it. She said Malcolm was perfectly capable of seeing to everything about the museum. She said she had been planning on closing it anyway, and now was as good a time as any."

"That's what I've been hearing all along," Priscilla said, "so I guess there's nothing odd about that." She didn't bring up their earlier conversation with Malcolm. She was sure Gerald had convinced him to settle with his aunt for whatever he had sold from the museum.

"I asked her about Cavanaugh," April continued. "She said she hadn't talked to him and, as far as she knew, he hadn't asked to see her. She was sure her attorney would have told her. I said it seemed likely that he was trying to keep a low profile while he was in Tisbury, so maybe he didn't want to talk to her attorney."

Priscilla frowned. "That seems strange. If he came to find something of his grandmother's he thought Malcolm or Katherine might have, why wouldn't he ask Miss Waterman? She's the one person the other two have in common."

"Maybe because he was already in contact with the house-keeper," April said.

"Did you ask her about Cavanaugh?"

"Yeah. She told me he hadn't been to the house. She didn't claim she hadn't talked to him, only that he hadn't been to the house. I didn't press. I didn't want her to think I suspected anything or to know I had heard about her meeting him in Oak Bluffs. She only said that if Mr. Cavanaugh wants something that belongs to his family, he'll have to talk to Miss Waterman about it. She's just the housekeeper."

"You didn't find out anything else?" Priscilla asked, giving Kitty an apologetic glance.

"No," April said. "I didn't like how that dog of theirs was always barking and growling and scratching at the door. Ms. Vaden had him shut in the kitchen. I thought maybe she was trying to hide something by claiming she had to keep the dog in there, but when I asked about it, she opened the door. The dog settled down when she told him to, and there was nothing to see. Just an ordinary kitchen."

"No sign of anything strange going on at all?" Priscilla asked.

"Nothing I could even begin to bring before a judge to get a search warrant. So I asked Miss Waterman if everything was all right and if she needed any help with anything."

"And?"

"She only laughed and thanked me. She said she was just fine, and I didn't need to keep checking on her. What can I say? She looks healthy and comfortable. No signs whatsoever of neglect or abuse. She did look a little uneasy the first time I came by and again at first this time, but a lot of people are that way with the police, even if they haven't done anything wrong. So if she's being blackmailed, she doesn't seem to want help with the situation. There's not a lot more I can do without proof."

Priscilla sighed. "I guess that's it, then."

"No," Kitty mouthed almost silently.

"She did look a bit wistful," April said. "Like she enjoyed the company, brief as it was, but you told me already she didn't want to see your friend Kitty or keep up correspondence with her, so maybe I'm wrong about that."

"Thank you for trying anyway," Priscilla said.

"I hope I've set your minds at ease, and we can put this to rest. Enjoy the rest of your visit with Mrs. Merrick."

Once the call was over, Priscilla spent the rest of the drive home filling Kitty and Gerald in on the conversation.

"I don't know what actual evidence you're going to find at this point," Gerald said. "Miss Waterman doesn't seem to want help. Malcolm says he doesn't know anything else about what Cavanaugh is after. Cavanaugh isn't talking. The housekeeper isn't talking. Aunt Katherine certainly isn't talking at this point."

"From what Kitty tells me," Priscilla said, "Katherine never wrote to her about Rosie Cavanaugh or any of the Cavanaughs in particular when she was alive. I can't see that we have anything to go on."

"Even if Anna is blackmailing Miss Waterman?" Kitty asked, her eyes pleading.

They were at the cottage by then, and Priscilla didn't answer. She turned to Gerald instead. "Thanks for helping us with Malcolm. I don't think he would have been that straightforward if it was only me and Kitty."

Gerald straightened his uniform with a satisfied smile. "The outfit helps, you know."

"I'm glad you're in a position to make him clean up the junk he threw in the water," Kitty said.

"All part of the job, ma'am."

Once they said goodbye to Gerald and went inside, Priscilla finally considered the question Kitty had asked earlier. Did they know for sure that Anna was blackmailing anyone? Did they know—really know—that she and Rowan Cavanaugh had met in Oak Bluffs?

"I don't know what to say about Anna, Kitty. We just don't have enough to go on." She gave her friend a sympathetic smile. "Come on. Jake wants to go for a walk."

Jake wriggled happily when he saw the leash, and soon they were outside again. The March air had turned cool, and the brisk walk felt good, but after a minute or two, Priscilla slowed her steps. Kitty's legs weren't very long.

"Sorry about that. I know I'm a fast walker."

Kitty smiled. "It would be nice to slow down some. Easier for me to think."

"What do you want to do? I realize you have a life to get back to. And, to be honest, I don't know if there's much more we can find out."

Kitty's eyebrows went up. "You're not saying you want to quit, are you?"

"No." Priscilla pretended to glare at her. "Bite your tongue. I'm just wondering what your husband and your boss are going to say if you stay out here much longer."

"I've been keeping in touch with them. Keith understands. If it wasn't for his own job, he'd be out here with me. My boss is okay for now too, though I don't think he's going to be very patient with me much longer. I have a pretty important client in a hurry to close, so once he and the buyer see to everything they have to do, the client is going to want me there to get everything finalized. For now, though, we're waiting on some things the title company has asked for. But, uh, maybe I ought to move to a hotel or a bed-and-breakfast or something. I know I've been a real imposition on you."

Priscilla rolled her eyes. "Just stop. It's been fun having you here, and I'm as interested as you are in finding out what's going on. I just don't know how practical it is, especially when we've come up with so little concrete evidence."

"But there has to be something. Remember what you said just a while ago about Malcolm trying to get back in touch with his aunt right after Aunt Katherine died? Okay, yeah, the timing could be coincidence. But what if it really *is* tied into all this? Maybe Aunt Katherine isn't still alive and in hiding, though I don't know if so far we've actually proved she isn't."

"Kitty."

"We ought to at least try to think of what other reasons Miss Waterman might have for not letting anyone into the house."

"But it has to be something she's decided to do because she wants to," Priscilla said. "Because she's mad at her family, like Malcolm said. Her lawyer comes to see her when necessary. I suppose her doctor does too. April's been there twice just recently. Anna didn't keep her from going where she wanted to. That doesn't seem to me like she's hiding something. If she is, she's hiding it in plain sight."

"But suppose Anna really is blackmailing Miss Waterman. If it's not because she knows where Aunt Katherine is, then what? And here's another question: If Mr. Cavanaugh is so determined to find whatever it is he's looking for, and he thinks Aunt Katherine might have either had it or known about it, why wouldn't he contact Miss Waterman? Wouldn't she be the first person he'd ask?"

"Unless he was depending on Anna to find out what he wants without being personally involved himself." Priscilla frowned. "I wish Miss Waterman would talk to us, just for a few minutes."

"I know. I'm sure I could get her to tell us what's going on."

Priscilla wasn't so sure about that, but she didn't say so. Instead she let Jake pull her along as he sniffed at cars and trees and barked at a squirrel that chattered at him from fifteen feet above their heads. They had just turned to go back to the cottage when Priscilla's cell phone rang.

"That's Joan," she said, smiling when she heard the tone, and then she answered. "Hey, Joan. What's going on?"

"I'm so sorry." Joan was in tears. "I just can't."

"What's wrong? Joan, are you okay? What's wrong?"

"I just can't keep this puppy."

CHAPTER FOURTEEN

W hat's wrong?" Priscilla repeated. "Joan. Tell me what happened. Are you all right? Is Sister all right?"

Kitty's eyes widened, and she looked questioningly at Priscilla.

"She's all right," Joan said. "I'm the one who's a mess. Can you come over? I really need to talk to you about this."

"Okay, sure. Kitty and I were just out walking Jake, but we're headed home. I'll be at your place in a few minutes." Priscilla nodded reassuringly at Kitty. "I'm glad Sister's okay."

"Oh." Joan took a shuddering breath. "I forgot you had company. Never mind. I'll figure this out."

"No, it's okay. Really. Just give me a few minutes. It's not a problem, I promise."

"If you're sure."

Joan sounded almost normal, but Priscilla could hear Sister whining in the background, probably from the confines of her crate. What had she done now?

"I'm sure," Priscilla said. "You just sit tight. I'll be right there."

"What happened?" Kitty asked once Priscilla ended the call.

"I hope you don't mind." Priscilla quickened her stride, making Kitty hustle to keep up. "I don't know what's going on with Sister, but Joan's very upset. You won't mind being on your own for a little while, will you?"

"Not at all. I can take Jake inside if you want. I need to check in with Keith anyway and with the office to make sure there's nothing I need to take care of, and then Jake and I will just watch a little TV."

"Thanks for understanding."

Priscilla let Kitty and Jake into the cottage and then hurried over to Joan's house. As she had suspected, Sister was in the crate and Joan was in tears.

"I've been trying," Joan said on a sob. "I really have. I know she's just a puppy and she doesn't understand. I just—just can't deal with this anymore. I'm sorry. It was very nice of you to give her to me. I know you meant well, but I just can't do it."

Sister whined from her crate, and Joan turned her face away.

"It's all right." Priscilla wrapped her arms around her cousin. "It's okay. I shouldn't have surprised you with a pet. That's never a good idea. I thought you really wanted one and just needed a little push. Did something happen to upset you?"

Joan's eyes filled with tears, and she walked over to the coat closet and took a box from the shelf. It wasn't a very large box, perhaps eighteen inches wide, two feet long, and six or eight inches deep. Joan sat with it on the couch.

"What it is?" Priscilla asked, sitting next to her.

Tears still running down her face, Joan removed the lid. Priscilla looked inside and wanted to cry too. These were Champ's things—his collar and his toys, the rubber duck and the stuffed squirrel Joan had been convinced he thought were real. In with everything else was a nearly shredded blue-and-brown flannel quilt, the quilt Champ had loved since he was a tiny puppy, the quilt Joan had clung to and wept over after Champ had died.

"Oh, Joan." Priscilla hugged her again. "I'm so sorry."

The puppy was looking forlornly through the bars of her cage, clearly not understanding why she had been confined.

"I know," Joan sobbed, clutching at what was left of the blanket, "I know she's only a baby and doesn't understand. I know it's only a worn-out old dog blanket. I know this shouldn't be a big deal."

"It is a big deal because of what Champ meant to you," Priscilla soothed. "I understand."

Joan didn't say anything else. She just sat and clutched the blanket.

"How in the world did Sister manage to get it?" Priscilla asked finally.

Joan drew a shuddering breath. "It was my fault. She had another accident, so I cleaned it up, and then we went for a walk. We had an awful time of it. If she wasn't trying to pull me off my feet, she was getting between them, and if not that, she was barking at everything she saw. And before you remind me that she's just a puppy, I know that very well."

"I know you do," Priscilla said quietly.

Joan calmed the slightest bit. "Anyway, when we got back, I was really missing Champ. He was always so well behaved. Never an accident, never a problem when we were out, never tore up anything in the house."

Priscilla wondered if Joan wasn't glossing over Champ's early days, but she didn't want to say anything aloud. "So what happened when you and Sister got home?" she asked instead.

Joan sniffled into a tissue. "Sister was in the kitchen eating, and I got down this box so I could look at Champ's things. Just to remember him. After a few minutes, the phone rang and I got up to answer it. It was some guy selling time-shares, and he wouldn't believe me when I told him I wasn't interested. When I finally hung up, I turned around and saw Sister with Champ's blanket in shreds all around her. I just couldn't take it anymore. I can't do this." She was sobbing again. "I'm sorry. I'm really sorry."

Sister whimpered from her crate, clearly wanting to go to Joan.

"Don't be sorry." Priscilla hugged her again. "I really do understand, and I know this is upsetting for you. Are you sure you want to give her back?"

Joan pressed the tear-soaked tissue to her mouth and nodded.

Sister still looked out of her cage, her dark, liquid eyes pleading, her little forehead furrowed with concern. According to the shelter, she had never been caged before. Of course, a crate was meant to be more of a den, a home, and not a cage, but Sister didn't look as if she thought of it that way just now.

"Can you keep her until tomorrow?" Priscilla asked. "I'll call the shelter and see what their policy is for returning dogs. Or would you rather I took her back to my house until I can take her back?"

Joan finally looked at the crate, and Sister pressed closer to the barred door, quivering as if she wanted to wag her tail but didn't dare to.

Joan sighed and shook her head. "I can keep her until you find out what we need to do. I know Jake probably wouldn't care for a strange visitor, even for a short time."

"Okay, if you're sure."

Joan nodded. "That'll be okay. And really, I'm sorry." She looked very composed now and very determined. "I just can't keep her. I'm sorry."

"No," Priscilla told her, "I'm sorry. I should have asked you first and believed you when you said you weren't ready. I'll call the shelter first thing tomorrow, and we'll get this straightened out. I'm sure somebody will want her. She's too cute to be at the shelter very long."

Joan softened slightly. "Poor little thing. She is awfully cute. I just..." Her lip quivered, and she drew a steadying breath. "Thank you for understanding."

Priscilla felt on the verge of tears herself as she drove back to the cottage. Maybe she was completely wrong, but she felt more strongly now than ever that Sister was precisely the right dog for her cousin. Clearly the puppy adored Joan, and she really was no more than a baby. She needed training, and there were bound to be mishaps, but she was eager to please and so full of love. Surely she deserved more than a few days to learn what Joan expected of her.

If only Sister had found something else, something less precious to Joan, to tear to bits. Maybe then Joan would have shrugged it off as she had Sister's earlier destructive antics. Clearly Joan was torn about her decision to give up the dog, but Priscilla hadn't wanted to try to discuss it with her when she was so upset over Champ's blanket.

Jake ran to greet her when she got home, tail wagging and tongue lolling in a wide doggy smile, and Priscilla bent down to hug him close.

Kitty looked up from the couch and closed her laptop. "How's Joan?"

"Not good." Priscilla went over and sat beside her. "Sister chewed up her other dog's blanket, the one Joan's saved since he died, and she's pretty upset. She wants me to take Sister back to the shelter."

"Oh, no. She can't really mean that. Sister's the sweetest thing. Why?"

"Joan says she can't deal with her. And it's true, puppies are a handful, and it takes patience and perseverance to train them so they're not a pain to live with. But I can't help thinking there's something else behind this. She's had puppies before. Champ was a puppy once. She knows what it's like." Priscilla sighed. "I guess that will teach me not to think I know what's best for someone else."

Kitty sighed. "And I don't have anything better to tell you. I talked to my boss. I have to go home. That closing I told you about has been pushed up at my client's request. He wants to get it done, and my boss has taken care of a lot of it for me already, but the client won't deal with anyone else as far as doing the actual closing. I can take care of some of it from here, but I have to get back, or the client is going to find somebody else to manage his real estate deals."

"That's not good."

"No. No buyer, no commission, no satisfied client, and no happy boss." Kitty sighed. "To be honest, I shouldn't have taken this much time already, but I was getting pretty burned out at work, and I just needed some time off. For me."

"That's understandable," Priscilla said. "I may be prejudiced, but Martha's Vineyard is a pretty nice place to relax in."

Kitty smiled. "It has been nice, thanks to you and your family and friends. I just hate to leave without really knowing what's going on here."

"I'm sorry about that. Sometimes it takes a while to figure these things out. And maybe there's just not that much to know."

"You don't believe that any more than I do," Kitty said. "But I guess I'll have to leave it up to you. Maybe," she teased, "you and your handsome sailor can solve the mystery."

"At least he helped us with Malcolm's part of it."

"It seems to me," Kitty said, "that Malcolm is as clueless about all this as we are. Well, I guess none of this is any of my business anyway. If Aunt Katherine knew something about the Cavanaughs and they don't want it getting out, I don't know what it is, and they can't get to her now anyway."

"So you don't really think she's still alive and in hiding."

Kitty shrugged. "I don't know what to think. Okay, yes, it's a pretty crazy idea, but there's something going on. I know there is. I just wish I didn't have to go home right away."

"Sounds like you have some pretty important business to attend to," Priscilla said. "And you do have to make a living."

"Yeah." Kitty grinned. "There's that."

"Did you book your flight?"

"Day after tomorrow. Ten fifty-five. We're still waiting on a few things before we can really get going on this sale, so I can stay at least that long. I know I've taken terrible advantage of your hospitality, but I wanted to give myself as much time here as possible, just in case something turns up. And if it doesn't, I can at least help you work on your lighthouse exhibits until I go. I know it's not much, but I don't know how else I can repay you for putting up with me and my crazy problem."

"You don't have to repay me at all. I've loved having you, and I don't think this problem is the least bit crazy. I do wish we had more answers. But even if you have to go home, I'll keep a lookout for anything I can find. I'm not giving up yet."

Kitty beamed at her. "I knew you wouldn't. And I'm not giving up either, even if all I can do is brainstorm with you over the phone from home."

"I'm glad you can at least stay through tomorrow. Maybe we'll turn something up by then."

"I don't guess it's very likely, but who knows?"

"And how's Keith?"

"He's the best guy in the world. We had a long talk while you were gone. I hadn't really expected to stay this long. Aunt Katherine was really Mother's friend, not mine. I was just planning to check on her and have a look around Martha's Vineyard. I never thought I'd spend more than a few hours here." Kitty smiled again. "But I didn't expect to run into you. I certainly didn't expect to get mixed up in some kind of mystery involving the Cavanaughs, of all people. I guess..." She grew serious again. "I guess I don't like the idea of Aunt Katherine or anyone else just disappearing without someone knowing what happened. What *really* happened. Maybe she was only a housekeeper with no family, but that doesn't make her any less valuable than Rowan Cavanaugh the Fourth."

Priscilla patted her arm. "Of course not. And if something happened to her because she just happened to get in some big shot's way, then someone should know about it. Just because she was elderly doesn't mean she was disposable."

"I've been thinking of something else," Kitty said, her serious expression turning troubled. "We've talked a lot about how the Watermans and the Cavanaughs were longtime friends and how Aunt Katherine worked for both families and probably knew a lot about their private matters."

Priscilla nodded.

"And Miss Waterman refused to reconcile with her nephew right after Aunt Katherine died."

"Yes, but—"

"I know she wasn't seeing anyone anyway by then," Kitty said, "but I'm thinking of what you said earlier. If Malcolm's right and it's because her family moved off and ignored her, you'd think she'd be eager to have one of them asking her for forgiveness and wanting to restore the relationship, wouldn't you?"

"Unless she was so mad at all of them by then that she didn't care if she ever saw any of them again."

"But let's suppose that's not the case," Kitty insisted. "Let's suppose something else happened right then, something to do with Mr. Cavanaugh and her new housekeeper and why she's selling her land and closing the museum and all those things. Something new."

Priscilla frowned. "Like what?"

"Suppose it wasn't Rosie Cavanaugh who had something to hide. Suppose Mr. Cavanaugh is trying to find out about something Rosie knew that would incriminate Miss Waterman."

"What do you mean?"

"I don't know. This sounds even crazier than all the other theories we've talked about, but what if Aunt Katherine knew something about Miss Waterman, maybe even something Rosie Cavanaugh told her years and years ago? And when Miss Waterman found out she knew, she didn't want it getting out, and she was afraid Aunt Katherine might talk."

Priscilla could manage only an incredulous little huff. "You mean murder?"

"Who was in the house when Aunt Katherine died?" Kitty asked. "Who reported the death? Who identified the body?"

"But really. Miss Waterman? From what April Brown said, she's just a frail old lady."

"And how hard would it be for a frail old lady to push another frail old lady down the stairs?"

Not that hard.

"But everybody claims they were best friends," Priscilla said. "She said as much in her letters to you, didn't she?"

"Yeah, she always said she and Miss Waterman got along well, and if they lived a quiet life, it was all right by her."

Priscilla thought for a minute. It was a bizarre idea, wasn't it? That nice old Miss Waterman would murder the only friend she had left? Still...

"I suppose they could have argued about something. Even best friends do that."

"True," Kitty said.

"Maybe before then, Miss Waterman didn't know your aunt knew whatever it is she's trying to keep quiet. Maybe your aunt just blurted it out because she was mad. I don't know. If that was the case, Miss Waterman could have gone after her right then. Or maybe she just waited until there was an opportune moment, when Katherine thought everything had blown over, and she could just give her enough of a shove to throw her off balance."

Kitty winced. "That's horrible."

"It is. It seems too outlandish to even be possible, but who knows what people will do if they think they have to."

"That would be something damaging enough to pay blackmail over," Kitty said. "If Anna found out about it after she came to work for Miss Waterman, that would explain the nice clothes and jewelry and everything else."

Priscilla nodded. "And she's certainly not going to be pushed down the stairs by frail little Miss Waterman either."

"It's horrible," Kitty repeated. "Just horrible."

"If only we could figure out what it is that Mr. Cavanaugh wants. That would settle all of this. Either it would give Miss Waterman a motive for murder or it wouldn't."

"If it does, whatever it is, is serious." There was deep concern in Kitty's dark eyes. "What do you think it could be?"

CHAPTER FIFTEEN

They ended up going back to the lighthouse and working more on the exhibits, proposing and dismissing theories about what Rowan Cavanaugh could have come in search of.

Kitty sighed and rearranged the eighteenth-century peacoat and cap to be displayed with the story of the early Lathams and their miniatures. "I know we don't have much to go on, but the idea that Miss Waterman might have murdered Aunt Katherine simply won't leave me alone."

"I know." Priscilla put down the paper towel she had been using to polish the glass on one of the display cases. "I wish you hadn't come up with it. How in the world are we going to find out exactly what Mr. Cavanaugh wants? He won't tell us. If Anna is getting paid by someone to keep her mouth shut about it, she won't tell us. And, of course, if Miss Waterman killed your aunt over it, she's not going to tell us either."

"Maybe the police—"

Priscilla held up her hand. "We can't ask April to go out there again. All we have is speculation, and she's stretched a point going out there twice already."

"But couldn't she talk to Mr. Cavanaugh? Just for a minute?"

"And what's she supposed to say to him? 'Tell me your guilty secret'? And that's all it would take to get the whole truth out of him?"

Kitty sat down and propped her chin in her hand. "But I only have one day left before I have to go home. Isn't there something we can do to at least try to figure this out before then?"

"I don't know what it would be."

Priscilla sympathized, she really did. She felt as frustrated as Kitty sounded, but figuring out what was going on had proved to be infuriatingly difficult. Something was wrong, that she was sure of, but what it could be she couldn't start to guess.

Kitty looked at her appealingly. "Maybe Miss Waterman—"

"We already promised we wouldn't bother her again."

"We told Anna Vaden that. But maybe Miss Waterman wouldn't mind company after all."

"Kitty! You just got through telling me she's a murderess, and now you want to go visit her?"

"Well, she was very nice when she was writing me, even if she was pretending to be Aunt Katherine."

Priscilla put her hands on her hips. "What are we supposed to do? Break into the house when the housekeeper isn't looking?"

Kitty looked defiant. "Maybe."

"Kitty!"

"Well, fine." Kitty huffed, her mouth turned down, her brow furrowed. "I think I'd better get back to my laptop. If I'm going to be a grown-up, I'd better see if there's anything my client needs right now and if there's anything else I can get done before I go home."

Priscilla decided to take a break as well and called the animal shelter to tell them about Sister. She was thankful that they agreed to take her back. The woman she spoke to was actually very understanding and said she was optimistic someone would adopt Sister right away. Priscilla was sure of that too, and it broke her heart. Sister was meant for Joan, she just knew it. She couldn't go somewhere else now. Who knew how another owner might treat her, and she was such a sweet-natured little thing.

Kitty spent most of the rest of the day dealing with her impatient client, calming her nervous boss, and trying to get the final pieces of information she needed to assure the coming closing would go as smoothly as possible. Priscilla, trying not to worry too much about what might happen to Sister, considered adding a fresh salad to what was left of the meatloaf and calling it dinner. Then she pinched the aluminum foil back into place over the pan and went into the living room.

"Come on," she said. "You've been working all day, and we haven't done very well with our investigating. I think we deserve some kind of treat."

Kitty looked up from her computer with a sigh and a tired smile. "It's okay. I had no business just showing up here like I did and expecting you to drop everything to try to figure out what happened to someone you'd never even heard of."

"You like lobster, don't you?" Priscilla gave her a mischievous smile. "Come on, I know you do."

Kitty laughed softly. "Okay, you know I do. But you have to let me buy. After all, you've let me stay here and—"

"Nope. It's my idea, so it's my treat. Are you at a stopping point?"

Kitty looked at her computer, clicked over to another screen, and then shut the whole thing down. "I am now. Do I need to dress up?"

"I wouldn't go there in a sweat suit, but I think what you have on is fine. I'm going to give my makeup a once-over, but I'll be ready to go after that."

"Okay, me too."

Kitty hurried to the guest room, looking much more cheerful than she had a minute earlier. Somehow Priscilla felt a little happier too, as she freshened up in front of her mirror. At least they could splurge one more time before Kitty left. Maybe it would get their minds off Mr. Cavanaugh and Miss Waterman and what could have happened to Katherine Evans.

They walked down the Harbor Walk toward the restaurant.

"You should see this place in the summer," Priscilla said. "It's full of all kinds of vendors and artists with their original creations and just a ton of things to do. You'll have to come back sometime. You and Keith. Wouldn't it be great?"

"It would." Kitty made a wry face. "Of course, I won't have any more vacation for a while, but I'll talk to Keith about it. I bet he'd love it here. And I promise we'll stay in a bed-and-breakfast."

Priscilla laughed and led her to the Lobster Shack. "Here we are," she said, opening the door. "What do you think?"

"Oh, it's nice. Not so fancy I don't feel comfortable but fancy enough to make me feel just a little bit spoiled."

"Perfect."

"Though this doesn't look like much of a 'shack.'" Kitty looked around the dining room, admiring the crisp white table-cloths and glistening crystal, the plush carpeting and gleaming cherry wood.

"Well, the cousins tell me that it didn't used to be much of a place, sort of like a mid-priced chain restaurant, but then it got a new owner. He wanted to have something a little nicer than usual right on the Walk, so he fixed up the Shack. I don't know what it was like before I moved here, but he must have done a great job of it."

A distinguished maitre d' sat them at a table with a lovely view of the sunset-gilded harbor, and Kitty sighed. "So beautiful. I can see why you wanted to come to Martha's Vineyard for good."

"It was an amazing opportunity," Priscilla admitted, "and I sure wasn't going to turn it down. Getting close to my family again was the best part, even without all the other perks. I really think it was a miracle. Just when I needed it most."

"I believe in miracles," Kitty said. "And we sure could use one right now."

"You know, it's funny you should mention that, but I've really been thinking about the sermon we heard on Sunday. About everything covered being revealed and everything hidden being shown."

"I always thought that meant at the end of the world."

Priscilla shrugged. "I suppose it does that too, but what if that's not *all* it means? What if it's also an encouraging word for us right now?"

"It still could mean we won't know about Aunt Katherine until the end of the world."

"Maybe so," Priscilla said with a laugh. "But maybe we should keep our eyes open all the same. Who knows? But for now, let's just enjoy our dinner."

There weren't many people in the restaurant yet, so their waiter was very attentive and their coffee arrived quickly. Kitty ordered lobster thermidor, lobster shells stuffed with cooked lobster in a white wine sauce, topped with parmesan cheese, and broiled to perfection, and Priscilla decided to try the lobster Colorado, bacon-wrapped filet mignon topped with lobster. Both dishes sounded delicious.

They talked and reminisced about old times and old friends, and Priscilla told Kitty more about her family in Martha's Vineyard.

"And you didn't know your cousins at all before you moved here?" Kitty asked.

"I had vague memories of them, from when I last visited here, but that was when I was eight. When I came back here to live, I couldn't have picked them out in a lineup."

"You seem so close now."

"We're getting there," Priscilla said, smiling at the thought of finally being close to her Latham relatives, but then her smile faded. "Obviously I don't know Joan as well as I thought I did."

"I'm so sorry it didn't work out with Sister. She's just adorable. I'm tempted to take her home with me."

"I wish you could." Priscilla bit her lip. "I'm just wondering if I ought to take her. I hate the thought of returning her to the shelter. I mean, the people there are very nice and take good care of the animals, but poor little Sister doesn't need to feel like she's lost another home, does she?"

"*Could* you take her? I'd feel better if you did too, but I'm not sure if that's something you'd want to do either. What would Jake think?"

"It's hard to say. I guess I could try it out. He seems pretty happy being an only dog right now."

"Maybe if you took her for a day or—" Kitty gasped. "Don't look."

"What?" Priscilla looked around the room, making sure not to move her head. "What is it?"

"It's Mr. Cavanaugh. He just came in. The maitre d' is fawning all over him."

Priscilla turned her eyes to the restaurant entrance. It was definitely Rowan Cavanaugh. "He looks like he's alone. I wonder why he's still in town."

"Because he hasn't found what he's looking for yet," Kitty whispered. "I wish we could talk to him."

Priscilla grinned, remembering that verse about hidden things being revealed. Maybe this was their opportunity. "I don't see why we can't." She smiled as Mr. Cavanaugh happened to look her way. Throwing caution to the wind, she stood and went over to him.

"Mr. Cavanaugh! You know, my friend Kitty and I were just talking about you and your family. We're sure there's a lot more you could tell us about the time her aunt worked for your grandmother."

"Well, I—"

"Won't you join us?" She took his arm, turning him toward their table, and then gave the maitre d' her most engaging smile. "It won't be a problem if he sits at our table, will it?"

"It's all right," Cavanaugh assured the man. "There's nothing I like better than getting a chance to chat with my friends all over the country."

The maitre d' gave a swift order to a passing waiter, and soon another place setting was laid between Kitty and Priscilla.

Mr. Cavanaugh sat down, ordered the specialty of the house, and then looked at them indulgently. "Well, I didn't really expect to see either of you again. Does this invitation mean you've remembered something Katherine Evans told you? Regarding my family?"

"I'm sorry," Kitty said, "but I haven't."

She gave Priscilla a slightly panicked look, and Priscilla smiled.

"As I said, Mr. Cavanaugh, Kitty and I were thinking that you might actually be able to help *us*. About her aunt Katherine."

"I believe I already told you that Ms. Evans worked for my grandmother before I was born. I never even met her. That's why I was hoping *you* could tell *me* something."

"Maybe if you told us exactly what you're looking for," Priscilla said as demurely as she could manage, "we could help you figure out where it is."

Kitty almost choked on her coffee.

Mr. Cavanaugh's eyes widened almost imperceptibly, and then that politician's smile curled the corners of his mouth. "You act like I'm looking for something in particular. As I recall, I merely asked Ms. Merrick here if her aunt had mentioned anything about my family or sent her any mementos. That seems fairly general, doesn't it?"

"True," Priscilla admitted, "but you just seem like you're after something." *Everything hidden is going to come out,* she reminded herself, and she looked Mr. Cavanaugh right in the eye. "Otherwise, why have you been meeting with Miss Waterman's housekeeper?"

"Her—" He smiled a little more stiffly now. "I don't recall mentioning that I had met with her housekeeper."

"No, but you have, haven't you?"

"What could she have to do with your grandmother?" Kitty put in. "She's only worked for Miss Waterman for a couple of years."

"Well, that is, of course, quite easy to explain, but how did you come to know that in the first place? I've been trying to keep a low profile while I'm here. You ladies must understand how it is for someone like me—people always wanting me to do something for them, see to something, sign an autograph. It can be very difficult to get anything done of a . . . personal nature."

He was stalling. Trying to think up something to say. A man like him was probably very good at stalling.

"You were seen," Priscilla said. "We just couldn't figure out what Anna Vaden could tell you about your grandmother." She gave him another guileless smile. "If there's some way we can help you with what you want to know and find out more about Kitty's aunt at the same time, we'd both be happy, right?"

"Of course."

There was a touch of amusement in his eyes now. Just enough to tell her he was onto her. Enough to let her know he hadn't been taken in by her offer to join forces with him.

"So why were you talking to Anna Vaden?" Priscilla asked. "If you don't mind my asking."

"Not at all. As you well know, Miss Waterman doesn't see anyone. Even the celebrated Rowan Cavanaugh the Fourth." He gave them a wry smirk. "I wrote to her lawyer, but the only answer she gave him to pass on to me was that she didn't know anything and did not choose to see me in person. So the next best thing was the housekeeper. She was, as you somehow know, good enough to meet me to discuss the matter. She promised she'd ask the old lady herself if there was anything she remembered about my family, but Miss Waterman didn't care to discuss it with her either." His mouth tightened. "It's very frustrating to know she's right there, someone who knew my family, was friends with my grandparents, and not be able to talk to her about them."

"Why don't you ask your own family?" Kitty asked.

He put on that slick smile again. "Sadly, most of the older generation is gone. Grandmother died rather young. Everyone who really knew her is either Miss Waterman's age or has already passed away. I have an Aunt Letty who knew Grandmother very well, but she's not well enough to discuss this sort of thing."

There was a sudden wariness in Kitty's expression, but she didn't say anything.

"I'm sorry to hear that," Priscilla said.

"Thank you," Cavanaugh said, "but it happens. Far too often, I'm afraid. One day I hope we'll have a cure or at least a treatment for dementia. For now, though..." He ended with a regretful sigh.

"I hope so too," Priscilla said quietly. "So there's no one left in your family who was close to your grandmother?"

"She and Miss Waterman were friends, but from what my father always told me, it was Katherine Evans who was closest to her, her maid and confidante. I would have loved to speak to her even for a few minutes. I'm sure she knew so many things about Grandmother that haven't come to light."

For there is nothing concealed that will not be disclosed..

"And you think she may have told some of those stories to Miss Waterman?" Priscilla asked.

"I don't know. They must have talked about Grandmother from time to time. I understand they spent a lot of time just passing the hours. It seems very likely they'd discuss a mutual friend, especially one they both loved dearly." He leaned forward just a little. "Or maybe Katherine might show her a souvenir my grandmother had given her at one time or other."

Just then, the waiter brought their entrées, and Priscilla was glad for the opportunity to think for a moment. Cavanaugh was definitely looking for something tangible, not just old reminiscences. But what was it?

The lobster and filet looked delicious, but Priscilla barely tasted them. Her thoughts were racing. So many questions. There was nothing to do but ask them.

"I'm curious, Mr. Cavanaugh," she said, making sure she expressed only a casual interest, "but why your grandmother in particular? From what I've heard, everyone in your family has led an interesting life. Your grandmother was herself quite celebrated in her day, and there have been many books written about her. Surely whatever you want to know would be easy to find out."

"I see you still don't understand, Mrs. Grant. My grandmother was just as you say, a darling of the press, a leader in society. And, yes, I could find out many things about her from books and other published items, but those would contain only the facts about her that I already know or, perhaps, some of the incidents her friends or family might have made public during and after her life. But those aren't the things I am most interested in. When she died, my father was a young man himself, so naturally he didn't know her or remember her as well as he did my grandfather. He couldn't tell me a lot about her, about the sort of things that wouldn't have been in the papers. I would just like to know if there's something about her, something *of* hers, that would possibly tell me more about the real person behind the personality. Is that so hard to understand?"

There was something very earnest in his expression now, something deeper than what he normally showed to the public. Something more real.

"No," Priscilla said softly. "No, I understand it very well. I'm really sorry we don't know anything or have anything that might help."

"But isn't there anything you remember your father saying about Aunt Katherine?" Kitty leaned forward in her chair, eyes eager. "Anything at all?"

"Believe me, I've tried to remember everything he ever told me about her. It never was much. She was just the maid, and he didn't really pay attention to her. Why should he?" Mr. Cavanaugh thought for a moment. "Just silly things. He got mad at my grandmother for telling Katherine about a girl he liked when he was in college, and Katherine went out and made him a pretty bouquet of Grandmother's roses to take to the girl the next day. He said Katherine was always thoughtful like that, and Grandmother told him not to worry about her telling anyone his secrets, that she had always trusted Katherine with her own."

Priscilla glanced at Kitty and then back at Mr. Cavanaugh. "You know, if she did know your grandmother's secrets, she can't tell them to anyone now."

"But she could have written them down somewhere." His face had lost its appealing softness. Now he looked like the ruthless politician some people believed him to be. "She could have whispered them in someone's ear or typed them into a computer. Who knows?" He fixed his eyes on Kitty. "She could have written them *to* someone."

Kitty looked as if she didn't dare move, didn't dare breathe.

"If she did," Priscilla said, "that someone wasn't Kitty."

Kitty nodded. "I–I told you, Aunt Katherine never even mentioned your grandmother to me. Or any of the Cavanaughs. I would have remembered that. And if she wrote anything to my mother about them, Mother never told me."

"I see. Well." Mr. Cavanaugh became the genial man of the people once more. "That's that, I suppose. But if by any chance you should remember anything that was said or come across a letter of your aunt's that mentions one of us, I would, of course, appreciate it very much if you brought it to my attention." He gave Kitty a business card with his contact information on it. "That's my private number and email address. No need for you to go through my office with something as trivial as this."

"I'm sure there isn't anything."

"But if there is," he pressed.

"I'll let you know. Do you want to look again at what Miss Waterman gave me?"

He shook his head. "That won't be necessary. Just remember to get in touch if you should remember anything." He gave Kitty his most engaging smile as he stood and laid several bills on the table. It was enough to cover their meals and whatever else they might order along with a generous tip. "I would certainly make it worth your while."

With that, he told them good night, and leaving most of his meal uneaten, he strode out of the restaurant.

CHAPTER SIXTEEN

O kay, that was a little scary," Kitty breathed once Mr. Cavanaugh was gone. "I know he didn't say anything, really, but he makes me nervous."

"I'm just glad you don't have whatever it is he's after. He looks like he would do just about anything to get his hands on it."

"Whatever it is," Kitty said.

Priscilla sighed. "Whatever it is. I'm more certain than ever there's something physical he's looking for. Or a clue to where it might be hidden right now. Too bad we don't know any more about what it is than we did before."

"Now what?" Kitty asked.

"Now I think we should finish this wonderful meal before it gets cold and then order some outrageously decadent dessert." Priscilla tapped the pile of bills in the middle of the table. "As long as Mr. Cavanaugh is buying."

Kitty checked her laptop when they got back to the cottage and found a few additional items she had to take care of before her client's closing. Priscilla took Jake for a quick walk while she worked, and then they all settled down to watch the first couple of episodes of the long version of *Pride and Prejudice*. It was a nice way to top off their evening of indulgence, and it was late when they finally went to their rooms.

Priscilla groaned when her phone rang very early the next morning. She recognized her cousin's ringtone.

"Joan." She cleared her throat, licked her dry lips, and then tried again. "Sorry. What's going on?"

"I can't find her." Joan sounded even more upset than she had the last time she'd called.

"What? What do you mean?"

"I can't find her," Joan repeated. "I can't find Sister. She was in the backyard, inside the fence, and I went into the house just for a minute. Just to go to the bathroom. I'd left her there for a few minutes before. I thought she'd be fine. And now she's gone. She's gone."

"It's all right." Priscilla swung her legs out of bed, went to the dresser, and started pulling out some clothes she could put on quickly. "She's got a chip, right? I can't remember if the shelter said she already has a microchip."

"No," Joan said, practically wailing. "Her paperwork says they highly recommend getting her chipped so she can be identified if she gets lost, but I didn't do it right away. And then when I thought—when I thought I wouldn't keep her, I decided I wouldn't bother with it. Oh, Priscilla."

"It's all right. It's all right. She can't have gone far. She's just a puppy."

"I don't know. There's the street and other dogs and wild animals—"

"Just give me a chance to get dressed," Priscilla said. "I'll be right over. You keep looking around and calling her."

"All right."

Once Joan hung up, Priscilla grabbed her robe and hurried over to the guest room.

"Kitty?" she called as she knocked. "Are you awake?"

"I am now," Kitty called back, and a few seconds later she opened the door. "What's wrong? Nobody calls this early unless there's something wrong."

"It was Joan," Priscilla told her. "Sister got out of the fence, and Joan can't find her. I told her I'd come over right away. I don't know if you want to—"

"Of course I'll come! That poor little puppy, she must be scared to death out there somewhere by herself. Give me a few minutes to get dressed. I'll be right out."

Before long, they were at Joan's cottage. Joan was standing out front, calling and whistling. She looked as if she was about to burst into tears. When she saw Priscilla, she did burst into tears.

"Oh, thank you for coming," she sobbed as Priscilla hugged her tightly. "I've got to find her. If anything's happened to her, I'll never forgive myself."

"It's all right," Priscilla soothed. "We're going to find her. What happened?"

Joan wiped her face with one hand, calming a bit. "She was in the backyard, like I told you. I guess Champ had tried to dig under the fence a few times. I had never noticed it before, and the hole was way too small for him to get out of, but Sister's so little, she just went right through. Poor baby. I'm sure she ran away because she thinks I hate her."

"I'm sure she doesn't think that," Priscilla said, hugging her again. "Puppies are just curious."

"I—I didn't hate her."

"Of course you didn't."

"I just—" Joan clung tighter. "I didn't want Champ to think I didn't love him. Or that I had forgotten him." Sobs shook her. "Or that another dog could take his place."

"Oh, Joan, of course not."

"I tried not to love her, and I wanted to so badly, and then I thought I'd better give her back before it was too late, and now it really *is* too late, and she's gone and I can't lose her now."

"It's all right." Priscilla squeezed her one more time and then let her go. "You're not going to lose her now. We're going to find her. She's just little. How far could she have gone?"

Joan wiped her eyes again and then smiled sheepishly at Kitty. "I'm usually not such a basket case. I'm sorry."

"Nothing to be sorry about," Kitty said, her eyes warm. "My cat accidentally got out a couple of years ago, and I was terrified. But we found her again. She was fine. I bet Sister will be fine too."

Joan smiled faintly. "Thank you for helping."

"Anytime. You and your family have been so nice to me. It's the least I could do."

"Trudy's on her way over, and so is Gail," Joan told them, still looking up and down the street for any sign of the puppy. "They're going to help look. Good thing Gail's boss was as understanding as mine."

"Do you want me to see if Gerald can help?" Priscilla asked.

"Do you think he would?" Joan asked, looking as if she might cry again. "Oh, that would be great."

"I'll give him a call."

By the time Gerald got there, Trudy and Gail had arrived too.

"I think the best thing we could do is split up into pairs and go different directions," Priscilla said.

Gerald nodded. "First, though, we'd better look all around the yard, front and back, and in anything Sister might have crawled into. Maybe she just got comfortable somewhere and fell asleep."

They looked everywhere a puppy could fit. They called and whistled and clapped and made every dog in the neighborhood bark and whine. They did not find Sister.

"All right," Gerald said, "I think it's time we split up and looked farther out."

"Priscilla and I can go this way," Kitty said at once, pointing toward the coast.

"All right," Priscilla agreed, not quite sure what Kitty was up to.

Joan looked hopefully at Gerald. "Can I go with you? I'm sure you've been all over this part of the island. Maybe you'd have some good ideas where Sister might be."

"Sure thing," he said. "If Kitty and Priscilla are going that way, I think we should head toward town."

"Okay," Gail said, "then Trudy and I will head over to those wooded areas two streets down and see what we find. We'll all meet back here. If you find anything, use your cell phone."

"We'll find her," Trudy assured Joan. "Don't worry!"

"Oh, wait." Joan rummaged in her pocket and brought out a bag of puppy treats. "You all had better take some of these, just in case she isn't sure she wants to go with you. If—if you find her, I mean."

"We're going to find her," Priscilla said. "We are."

The three groups headed in three different directions. Kitty walked swiftly toward the coast and then turned at the street corner. She scanned the yards they passed, still whistling and calling, but she was making a beeline for somewhere. That was pretty obvious.

"What are you up to?" Priscilla panted a little, struggling for once to keep up with her friend.

"I just thought this might be a good place to look." Kitty smiled innocently and started walking a little faster.

They turned onto the next street, and Priscilla stopped. "You're kidding me, right?"

"What do you mean?"

"This is the way to Miss Waterman's house. How do you even know that?"

Kitty's mouth tightened. "I looked it up. There are plenty of online maps. Besides, property is my job. I know how to find what I'm looking for."

"Just what do you think you're going to do? We already said we wouldn't come back. What are you going to say?"

Kitty huffed. "Look, this is my last day here. Tomorrow morning I'll be on a plane heading back to the West Coast. This is the only chance I'm likely to ever have to find out what's going on here and whether something bad happened to Aunt Katherine."

Kitty could be a little bulldog when she wanted to be. Priscilla remembered that from their days in Kansas, but she had never seen her quite so daring before.

"But what are you going to do?" Priscilla shook her head, and a conspiratorial smile touched her lips. "What are *we* going to do?"

"Well, we're going to look for Sister. That's first. But I don't guess it will hurt to search in the direction of Miss Waterman's house and just see what we see. Maybe you're right, and something that's been hidden will be uncovered."

Priscilla said nothing for a moment more. Exactly what were they going to do?

"All right," she said at last. "But we're not going to do anything crazy, okay? Just look, right?"

"Right."

There was a spark of excitement in Kitty's eyes, and Priscilla wasn't at all sure that same look wasn't in her own. A touch of intrigue, more than a bit of uncertainty and, yes, some fear. But she could be brave when she needed to. Couldn't she?

They kept calling and searching, stirring up the dogs they passed, sometimes scaring up a stray dog or cat or a squirrel or two. Before long they were in an empty lot that overlooked the back of the Waterman house. They both came to a stop in the shade of a large oak, simply watching. For several minutes nothing stirred, and then there was some movement in one of the upstairs windows. They both noticed it, but neither of them said anything. Then it was still again.

"Do you think that's her room?" Kitty whispered.

"That would be my guess," Priscilla whispered back, though there was no chance they could be heard at this distance. "Somebody's home, anyway."

"She's always home," Kitty reminded her.

They watched for a minute more, and then someone came out of the house and got into the Eldorado parked out front.

"That's Anna," Kitty whispered, and Priscilla nodded, shrinking back into the shadow of the tree branches.

The Eldorado drove away, and Kitty grabbed Priscilla's arm. "Come on."

"What are we going to do?" Priscilla asked, pulling back to slow her down. "What are you thinking?"

"We're never going to get a better chance. Anna's gone. Miss Waterman is up there alone."

"You think," Priscilla said.

"Who else?" Kitty's eyes lit. "Unless Aunt Katherine really is somewhere in there."

"Kitty!" Priscilla put her hands on her hips. "Neither of us knows who or what's in that house, and it's none of our business."

"But we could just go ring the doorbell and see, right? There's nothing against the law about that."

"But the housekeeper's gone. There's nobody to answer the door."

"There's Miss Waterman."

Kitty took off toward the house again, and Priscilla hurried after her. "She might not even be able to get downstairs. Then what?"

"We can just ring and see what happens."

They trudged through the weeds and tall grass until they reached the side of the house. There was nobody around. The street was quiet.

When they got to the corner of the house, they both peered around to the front, making sure no one was waiting for them. They crept up to the door. Priscilla was sure her heart was going a mile a minute.

Kitty looked at her, both eyebrows raised, and Priscilla shook her head. "This is your party. You ring the bell."

"Fine." Kitty thrust out her chin, straightened her shoulders, and reached out to ring the bell. Then she drew back her hand and looked at Priscilla.

"Well, go on," Priscilla said.

Kitty shook her head. "I think it's open."

"What?" Priscilla looked closer. It was true. The door was only pulled to. It wasn't even latched. "We'd better get out of here."

"No," Kitty urged. "We can't leave now. What if Miss Waterman is up there alone and someone else comes in? A burglar or something? What if Mr. Cavanaugh tries to come in and make her give him whatever it is he thinks Aunt Katherine had?"

"Kitty . . ."

"I'm going in."

Priscilla grabbed her arm. "You can't go in. It's breaking and entering."

"It's not breaking and entering," Kitty said, shaking free. "It's just entering. And if anybody asks, we came by to see if they had seen Sister and found the door open and wanted to make sure Miss Waterman was okay."

Priscilla exhaled. "I think this is the crazy part we weren't supposed to do."

"Stay out here if you want," Kitty said, lips pursed. "I'm going in."

She pushed the door with one finger, and it swung silently open. A superior smile on her lips, she stepped over the threshold. Priscilla followed her and pushed the door closed again.

They hadn't had more than a glimpse of the foyer's elegant wallpaper on their previous visits. Now a living room filled with antiques and fine works of art opened before them, and there was the sweeping stairway that led to the upper floor. Kitty looked at it and then uncertainly at Priscilla. Was this where Katherine Evans had died?

They took a few steps toward the stairs, and just as Priscilla was about to ask if anyone was home, there came a deep growl from under the white-brocade sofa.

The dog.

They had forgotten about the dog.

CHAPTER SEVENTEEN

Kitty gave a little shriek as the German shepherd charged out at them, blocking their way back to the front door.

For an instant, Priscilla froze. Then she made her face stern. "Sit."

The dog stopped, looking at her warily.

"I said *sit*."

Heart racing, she pointed at the floor, making sure to show no sign of weakness. To her astonishment, the dog obeyed. She didn't dare look back at Kitty, but she knew her friend was shrinking behind her, her breath coming in little gasps.

Remembering the puppy treats in her pocket, Priscilla tossed one at the German shepherd's feet. "Good dog."

The dog snapped it up and then looked at her, looking hungry and pitifully eager for praise.

"Good dog," she said again, looking around for a likely place to shut the dog in. There was a door on the other side of the stairway. Did it lead to the dining room? The kitchen? It didn't matter. It would have to do.

"Good dog," she repeated, making her voice syrupy. "You're a good dog."

She tossed down another treat, this one a little bit closer to the door she was aiming for. The dog took a couple of steps forward and ate the treat, again looking up for her approval.

"Now sit. Sit. Yes, good dog. Very good dog."

That was answered with obedience and the heavy thump of the dog's tail. Her heart was still in her throat, and she didn't dare take her eyes off the animal. With Kitty as her shadow, Priscilla moved closer to the door and dropped another treat.

"Come on. Good boy."

They finally reached the door, and Priscilla pushed it open. It was a dining room. There was another door at the back of it, presumably leading to the kitchen, but it was closed. This was perfect.

"Good dog," she said again. "Come on now. Good dog."

She tossed four or five of the puppy treats inside, and the German shepherd trotted after them, snapping them up as he had the others. As quickly as she could, Priscilla shut the door behind him.

Letting out a shaky breath, she sank into the overstuffed armchair that sat nearby, wondering if, for the first time in her life, she might faint.

Kitty still clutched her arm. "How in the world did you know to do that? How did you even have time to think what to do?"

Priscilla laughed breathlessly. "I was sure if we ran, he'd be on us. The only thing I knew to do was to act like I was the boss." She closed her eyes, panting and thanking God it had worked.

"What do we do now?" Kitty asked in a small voice.

The dog was whining and pawing at the door. Whether it wanted to get at them or just have another treat, Priscilla wasn't sure, but she knew if they wanted to actually talk to Miss Waterman, they'd better do it quickly, before Anna Vaden came back and caught them.

She forced herself to stand and made her voice sound steadier than she felt. "Well, we're in. We might as well do what we came here to do."

She looked up the gracefully curving stairway, trying not to think of Katherine Evans. Beside her, Kitty was looking up too, her usually rosy cheeks redder than usual.

Priscilla grabbed her arm, not sure which of them she was trying to calm. "Well, here we go."

There wasn't a sound in the house besides the occasional whining and scratching of the dog.

"Hush," Priscilla said, her tone very firm.

There was immediate silence, a silence that made her wish she hadn't said anything, a silence that made little shivers trickle down her spine. Miss Waterman was upstairs, wasn't she?

They started up the stairs, taking every step warily, jumping when one stair gave a loud creak and then smothering nervous laughs at their fright. *It's a perfectly normal house*, Priscilla reminded herself as they kept going upward. *There aren't going to be skeletons and ghosts around every corner.* Still, she felt as she had when, years ago, she had gone through a wax museum's "House of Horrors" all by herself. She couldn't have been inside it more than five minutes, but that five minutes had seemed like hours as she hurried past scenes of terror and figures of movie monsters, past and present, almost certain one of them was going to leap out at her. *Just a normal house*, she told herself again.

Finally they were at the top of the stairs, and Kitty clutched her arm once more, this time more tightly than ever. "What now?" she breathed, her voice scarcely a whisper.

Resisting the urge to remind Kitty that this had been her idea in the first place, Priscilla nodded toward the hallway. Except for one at the very end, the doors were open, sunlight streaming through them and onto the lush carpet. They glanced into the rooms as they passed. Still. Empty. Well kept, nicely decorated, but no sign of use. A lovely and empty shell.

Priscilla hesitated at the closed door at the end of the hallway.

"What if it's locked?" Kitty whispered.

Priscilla swallowed hard. "I guess we'll knock."

There was some noise from downstairs, the dog whining and scratching again, reminding her they'd better not stay long. Priscilla took a deep breath and then tapped on the door.

"Miss Waterman, are you in there?" There was no answer, so she tried the doorknob. It turned easily, and she pushed the door open about halfway. "Miss Waterman?"

The room was large and elegant, dominated by a canopied four-poster bed that looked at least a hundred years old. Light streamed in from the lace-curtained bay windows on either side of it. Across from them, in the shadowed side of the room, was a chaise lounge covered in antique gold brocade. On it, a frail, elderly woman sat with a crocheted afghan pulled up to her chin, looking over it at Priscilla and Kitty with frightened eyes.

"What do you want?" The woman's voice was thin and unsteady. "Who are you? My housekeeper will be back any minute."

"We're not going to hurt you, Miss Waterman." Priscilla stepped into the room. "We just wanted to make sure you were all right and talk to you for a few minutes."

"The girl from the police has been here twice already," the old woman said, a touch of imperiousness now in her voice. "I told her I was fine."

"We know. We just thought we could talk to you for a few minutes."

Kitty peeked around Priscilla's shoulder. "We didn't break in. The door was open."

Seeing her, the woman started and shrank back more deeply into her afghan, pulling it up to her nose. "You need to speak to my lawyer. He handles everything for me. I really—"

She broke off at the sound of a dog barking, at the thud of paws and the thump of footsteps, at the creak of the stair halfway up. Then Anna Vaden appeared in the doorway, holding the German shepherd by the collar as it growled at them.

"I thought as much," she snapped. "I saw the two of you back there, watching the house, waiting for me to go out so you could break in."

Kitty scowled at her. "We didn't—"

"Oh, I know. I figured you'd come in if I left the door open for you. I don't know how you got up here." She gave the dog's collar a harsh shake, making the beast growl more. "Stupid thing. I should have known I couldn't trust him to take care of business for me." She smiled coldly. "But you won't be able to distract him now."

"What are you going to do?" Priscilla asked, amazed that her voice sounded calm and steady and didn't betray the wild thumping in her heart.

"I told you both that Miss Waterman didn't want to see you, and I told you on more than one occasion. It's a pity you didn't listen to me. And it will be a pity when I have to tell the police that Rex here mistook you for burglars while I was out. Get 'em, Rex." Again she shook the dog's collar, and again the dog growled, lunging forward, hampered only by her hold on it.

"Priscilla," Kitty breathed, her face white.

Priscilla didn't move, couldn't move. Yes, she had managed the dog earlier, but now its true pack leader was here. Obviously Anna had trained it to attack at her command. It wasn't very likely to obey a mere stranger in her presence. Certainly not for puppy treats.

"Priscilla," Kitty whimpered.

Priscilla lifted her chin. "You can't—"

"Get 'em," Anna said, and she opened her hand.

Snapping and growling, the dog plunged forward.

"Rex! Sit!"

With a little yelp, the dog sat, expressive eyes going to the lady on the chaise. Miss Waterman smiled and patted the cushion beside her.

"Good boy. There's my Rex. Come on now."

The German shepherd trotted to her, eyes eager, tail wagging, and sat at her feet.

Anna's face was paper white as she stood gaping at the dog and the old lady. Then she finally collected herself. "Rex!" she snapped. "Come here! Heel! Heel!"

The dog looked at her warily and then leaned into the old lady's legs, looking up for approval.

"Good boy," Miss Waterman said, patting his head. "You should have used kindness instead of punishment, Anna." She glanced furtively at Priscilla and Kitty. Then she stroked the dog again and was rewarded with a look of adoration. "He was easy to win over," she said, her gently lined face turning grim. "I thought maybe it would help me escape."

"Escape?" Priscilla and Kitty said at the same time.

The housekeeper gave her a withering glare. "You'd better not say things you don't mean, Miss Waterman. People will get the wrong idea."

The old lady looked at her, defiance in every trembling line of her body.

"Be reasonable, ma'am," Anna tried again. "If you needed help, you might have easily said so to the lady from the police department." She looked at Priscilla and Kitty with a desperate smile. "She's getting a little forgetful these days, and a little fanciful. You know how old folks are. She's—"

"That's enough, Anna." The lady was clearly in possession of her faculties. "I'm done with this. I'm done with all of this."

The housekeeper's eyes filled with rage and hatred, but she nodded. "All right, Miss Waterman. If there's nothing more…"

She began to back out the door, but Miss Waterman stopped her. "I don't think so. I know it would be very easy for you to go down those stairs and straight out that door, but I don't think you ought to do that. You stay right here until we figure out what to do with you."

For an instant, Anna looked as if she might snicker at the threat, but then she saw the look on the old woman's face.

"Come over by the wall, away from the door," Miss Waterman ordered.

Anna did as she was told.

"Watch her, Rex." The lady patted the dog again and used a piece of cheese off a tray beside her chaise as a reward. "Watch her."

Anna took a step back, but the dog immediately barked and then growled. Her mouth in a hard line, Anna stood where she was.

Priscilla let out the breath she hadn't realized she was holding. "You know, Kitty, all this was your idea, and I…"

She trailed off when she saw what was in Kitty's expression: confusion, disbelief, shock… recognition. Then it was as if a light had been switched on. Miss Waterman was—

"Aunt Katherine!" Kitty gasped, and she took a step closer to the old lady, peering at her, half smiling. "You are Aunt Katherine, aren't you?"

Priscilla could see now the resemblance between the woman in the chair and the woman in the photograph she'd been shown. Not the woman she'd been told was Caroline Waterman, but the other one, her housekeeper and companion, her friend. Katherine Evans.

The old lady reached both hands out to Kitty, weary tears filling her eyes. "Yes. I'm so sorry. I'm so sorry about everything. I'm so sorry."

"It's all right." Kitty went to her, taking her hands and then hugging her trembling shoulders. "Everything is going to be all right."

Miss Waterman—Aunt Katherine—pulled an old-fashioned linen handkerchief from the pocket of her housedress and dabbed at her eyes. "I didn't think it would end up this way."

"What happened to Miss Waterman?" Priscilla asked as gently as she could, and from her place by the door, Anna snorted.

Katherine started to cry again. "She's dead. She died more than two years ago."

Kitty hugged her more tightly, making little soothing sounds.

Anna sneered at the old woman. "Mighty suspicious if you ask me, that death."

CHAPTER EIGHTEEN

Katherine's red-rimmed eyes were fierce. "I don't care what you tell them, Anna Vaden. I'm glad it's over. You go ahead and tell them whatever you want about murder and every other nasty thing you can think of. I can tell them about your blackmail, and I have records to prove everything I ever paid you." She looked frightened but somehow confident too.

"I think you'd better sit down, while she tells us what happened," Priscilla told Anna, indicating a ladder-back chair in the corner farthest from the door.

Anna looked down at the dog and didn't move.

Katherine's sobbing turned into low laughter. "Come on, Rex. Come on, baby."

The dog trotted to her, tail wagging, and Anna trudged over to the chair and plopped herself down, arms crossed and mouth set in a hard line. At Katherine's command, the German shepherd went to stand beside her, eyes fixed on her, waiting for a sign of movement.

"What happened?" Priscilla asked again, pulling another chair up next to the chaise and sitting down.

Katherine drew a trembling breath and then released it. "It was so horrible. I'd worked for Caroline for so long that we were more friends than employer and employee. We liked living quietly, playing cards and dominoes, watching movies, reading, sewing, those kinds of things. Caroline never heard from her family. She got tired of sending birthday presents and Christmas presents and never getting even a thank-you in return. She said the young ones would just send her a list of what they wanted, and after a time, they just asked for money. The older ones were slightly less blatant about it, but they never called, never wrote, unless there was something they needed from her. Malcolm, her nephew, was a little better, even though she had to bribe him to keep the museum running. But then they had a blowup over some girl he thought he was in love with, and he said he'd never be back either."

"Can you tell us about when she died?" Priscilla pressed.

"I'm getting to that. You won't understand anything unless you know the reason we did what we did."

"I'd say the reason's pretty plain," Anna spat. "You killed her and took her place. Living like a queen, all high and mighty, and sure nobody'd know the difference. Well, you didn't count on Anna Vaden, did you?"

Katherine looked into Kitty's eyes. "It wasn't like that. It wasn't like that at all."

"No," Kitty soothed, "of course not."

"I didn't want her money. I didn't need her money. I just wanted to finish my life without having to struggle for every penny. I didn't need to own a house or car or anything, and she didn't mind sharing what she had with me. I was getting too old to do much of the housework, but she didn't mind. There was a service that came in to do that. Like I said, we were friends. Nobody gave two hoots for either of us, but we were fine with that. But then . . . "

Tears filled her eyes again, and Kitty hugged her closer. "It's all right. *Shh*."

Katherine pressed her wadded handkerchief to her mouth. "It was late one night. We had just finished watching Errol Flynn in *Robin Hood*, one of our favorites. I took our empty popcorn bowls down to the kitchen to rinse them out, and I heard an awful clatter on the stairs. I ran back into the living room as quickly as I could, and Caroline was lying there on the floor." She closed her eyes for a moment, unable to speak.

"You don't have to tell us all this right now," Priscilla said. "If it's too difficult . . . "

Katherine shook her head. "I thought she was dead already, she looked so awfully white, and her nose was bleeding. But she opened her eyes when I got to her. I told her not to move, that I would call the ambulance, but she only smiled a little. 'I know I'm dying,' she said. 'I know, and it's all right. The Lord has a place waiting for me.' I told her she didn't need to worry about that quite yet, that when the ambulance came, they'd get her all fixed up, but she didn't believe me. I don't know. Do you think sometimes God makes us ready when it's time?"

"I hope so," Kitty said.

Katherine blew her nose. "Anyway, she said she wasn't worried about anything but what might happen to me. 'Your husband died years ago, you don't have any family. What will you do? Where will you go?' I told her I'd be fine, and she said she had always meant to do something for me in her will, she'd just never gotten around to it. All this was her idea. She said nobody would know the difference between two old ladies nobody ever saw. She said it wouldn't hurt her family in the least to wait a few years for the money they were after, that I should stay here, pretend to be her, and enjoy the house and whatever else I wanted until my time came. She said it was the least she could do for me after I'd taken such good care of her for so long. I told her I couldn't do it, that I'd never be believed, but she made me promise. I told the 911 operator that I was Caroline Waterman and that my house-keeper had fallen down the stairs, and somehow he believed me. Everyone believed me. I—"

She broke down again, and Priscilla reached over to take one frail hand. "It's going to be all right. You can tell the police every-thing. They'll understand."

Again Anna snorted. "The police will see right through that sob story in five seconds. Murder is what it was." She leaned for-ward in her chair aggressively, and the dog stiffened, growling low until she sank back again and was still.

"She's the one who made me put the property up for sale," Katherine said evenly. "Anna. I haven't spent any of the money except just enough to live on and for her demands, and I kept records of all of it."

"Good." Priscilla looked at Anna, who merely glared back at her. "The police will want to see that."

The glare grew more murderous, but the housekeeper said nothing.

"And I'm sure they'll be interested to know what you were meeting Mr. Cavanaugh about," Kitty added.

"He said he asked you to talk to Miss Waterman about things she might have that once belonged to his grandmother," Priscilla said. "What did you give him?"

"I didn't give him anything." Anna tightened her mouth and turned her glare on Katherine. "And I asked about the stuff. If she says I didn't, she's lying and she knows it."

"She did ask," Katherine said. "Or I should say, she demanded. But I told her what she told you, that I didn't have anything of the Cavanaughs' except what was in the museum. The stuff I had that was mine . . ." She smiled at Kitty. "I wanted you to have something to remember me by. I thought it was so wonderful of you to try to come see me and to care about what had happened to me." She hugged Kitty again. "You're so like your dear mother."

"I'm so glad you're all right," Kitty said.

Tears came into the old woman's eyes again. "I so wanted to see you that first time you came. I almost ran down the stairs after Anna to keep you from going away, but I knew I'd never make it before you were gone, and then it was too late."

"Why didn't you tell Officer Brown everything when she came to see you?" Priscilla asked. "She could have helped you."

"You mean the girl from the police?" Katherine shook her head. "I was so afraid. Anna's been telling me for two years that if I didn't do what she said, she would tell everyone I murdered Caroline so I could take her money." Her voice quavered. "I still don't know what they'll do to me, for lying about being her, but I didn't kill her. She was the best friend I ever had."

"I think they'll understand," Kitty told her.

"Today, though," Katherine said, "I couldn't let her set the dog on you." She looked again at Anna. "Keeping him hungry to keep him mean only made it easier for me to get him to trust me instead of her. First it was just because I was afraid of him, but then we got to be friends, didn't we, boy?"

The German shepherd gave a happy bark and thumped his tail.

"Still," Katherine said, "I wasn't sure what he'd do when she was around. She told me he was trained to kill if she wanted him to, and I didn't know what to believe. But I couldn't let him hurt you girls. Thank God he listened to me and not her."

"I wouldn't have let him hurt anyone really," the housekeeper muttered unconvincingly. "I just had him around to scare folks off. He wouldn't hurt a fly."

She reached over as if she'd pet the dog, and he growled low in his throat. She quickly put her hand back in her lap.

Priscilla eyed her coolly. "You never said what you were meeting Mr. Cavanaugh about in Oak Bluffs."

"He just had questions. I told him I'd ask 'Miss Waterman.' That's all there was to it."

"Then why couldn't he ask you those questions here?" Kitty asked. "Why did you have to go to Oak Bluffs to talk?"

Anna stuck out her chin. "It was his idea, so maybe you'd just better ask him."

"She's lying," Katherine said. "I heard her talking to him over the phone. She told him if he wanted her to look for anything else, they'd better meet somewhere and talk it over."

"Shut your mouth!" Anna half rose, but the dog barked and bristled, and she huddled in her chair again, dark murder in her eyes.

"Anything else?" Priscilla looked from Katherine to Anna. "You really might want to think about what you say right now. It might make a big difference in whether or not Mrs. Evans tells the police about everything you've been doing. Besides the blackmail, there's elder abuse, terroristic threat, kidnapping. I really can't say what kind of charges might be brought against you, but I'm sure Mrs. Evans might take it into consideration if you were to tell us what you were supposed to look for, and what you told him you'd found already."

Anna closed her lips tightly.

"Don't think Mr. Cavanaugh is going to get you out of this," Priscilla said. "Whatever it is, he can't afford to be involved, not if whatever you sold him is as sensitive as he acts like it is."

"He can pull strings," Anna said disdainfully. "If he doesn't, I can make him sorry he didn't."

She wouldn't say anything more after that. Priscilla used the telephone on the nightstand to call April Brown.

"It's Priscilla Grant again. Look, can you and maybe another of your officers come out to the Waterman house right away?"

"I already told you I'm not going back out there without evidence." There was nothing but exasperation in April's tone. "I don't think that housekeeper of Miss Waterman's will even let me inside the door again."

"I don't think she'll have much to say about it now."

"What are you talking about? What's going on?"

"Well," Priscilla said, smiling at Katherine, "we've found out exactly what happened to Katherine Evans."

"What do you mean?" April said. "She's dead."

"She's sitting on a chaise lounge up in Miss Waterman's bedroom right now. I'm looking straight at her."

April and Officer Rogers, a young man with earnest brown eyes, showed up a few minutes later. They listened as, with Kitty and Priscilla sitting on either side of her, Katherine told her scarcely believable story.

"I have a picture of Aunt Katherine and Miss Waterman back at Priscilla's cottage," Kitty added. "I'll be happy to let you see it. You can see they looked a lot alike when they were younger, but you can tell this isn't Miss Waterman."

"This is going to take a lot of sorting out," April said, "especially with the Waterman family. They may not take too kindly to you spending all of Miss Waterman's money and trying to sell off her property."

Katherine sighed. "It seemed like such a harmless thing to do at the time, especially with poor Caroline telling me it was what she wanted. How could I tell her no with her lying there dying? And it was so easy. Nobody ever had a question."

Priscilla didn't say it aloud, but she was certain they were all thinking the same thing: *Who would ask questions about an elderly nobody who had no one in the world to care about her?* It was too sad.

April fixed her eyes on the housekeeper, who hadn't said a word since her arrival. "And just how did you come into this, Ms. Vaden?"

Anna's only reply was an extremely disdainful look.

"I had to have someone look after things here," Katherine said. "Caroline always had someone, and it would have looked strange if she was suddenly here alone. I got Anna through an agency, and everything was all right for the first month or two. Then she realized I wasn't Caroline Waterman. She saw that photograph I sent you, Kitty, the one of me and Caroline at the banquet, and figured it all out. She'd been snooping around the house and found other pictures of Caroline, from events she attended years ago, and realized I didn't look exactly the same. I tried to pass it off as just my being older now, but she said she knew I was the woman in the photo with Caroline, not Caroline herself. She demanded to know what I'd done with Caroline, and I told her what happened. It sounded so awful, so unlikely, that I believed her when she said I'd be charged with murder and theft and all kinds of horrible things if she went to the police."

The disdain in Anna's expression turned colder.

"After that, it was awful," Katherine said. "She got that poor dog when she knew I was terrified of them to start with, and she told me he would attack me if I tried to leave when she was out. Before Caroline passed on, we had Elliot, the biggest, sweetest old tomcat, but he was nearly twenty and died before she did. I didn't know anything about dogs."

"Aww," Kitty murmured.

"Anyway, then Anna made me start paying her to keep her from telling the police what I'd done. It wasn't that much to start with, but then she got impatient and told me that she'd go away and leave me alone if I'd pay her one lump sum. She knew the property and the house where the museum is would set her up in style, so she told me to sell them. I didn't dare tell her no, but I knew we were talking about a lot of money, especially with property like that. I was going to try to escape and just disappear somewhere so she couldn't get her hands on everything."

April looked at her gravely. "It might have been better if you had—"

"I know. I know. It was crazy. All of this is crazy. I don't know how I even got myself into this mess. What can I do now but try to set things right?"

"I have a feeling this is going to take a while to straighten out. I'm not sure what the DA will want to charge you with. I guess that might depend on what the Waterman family wants to do."

Katherine drew a deep breath. "I won't fight them. They have every right to press charges for what I've done as much as for what Anna's done."

Anna glowered at her.

April's stern expression softened. "I don't think you need to worry too much quite yet, Mrs. Evans. As long as you don't go anywhere without letting me know, I suppose it won't hurt anything for you to stay right here for now."

Katherine gave her a whimsical smile. "Where else would I go?"

"You can stay with me and Kitty if you want to," Priscilla said. "We won't mind, will we?"

"Oh, it would be so sweet," Kitty said, squeezing the old lady's hand. "You will, won't you? Then you won't have to stay here by yourself, and we can look after you. Please do."

"But what would I do with Rex? I can't just leave him here alone." The dog looked at her when he heard his name, and she smiled sadly. "As fierce as he seems, he's really just a big baby."

"If you're unable to keep him," Rogers said, "the shelter—"

The shelter. Priscilla had forgotten all about Sister and everyone looking for her. Her phone hadn't rung. It seemed like a long time for them to still be searching. She'd have to call Gerald once April was gone.

"No. No, I couldn't possibly take Rex to a shelter," Katherine said, looking regretfully at Kitty. "You're both so kind, but I couldn't do it. I guess he and I will stay here until I can find us someplace else to go."

"Well, what if I stayed here with you?" Kitty said. "Would that be all right?"

"Your flight is at ten fifty-five in the morning," Priscilla reminded her. "And you really do have to go this time."

"I know. That's why I want to stay here as long as I can." Kitty looked pleadingly at April. "That wouldn't hurt anything, would it? Just until I have to leave."

April's mouth tightened, but it was obvious she was trying not to look too soft. "I'll get in touch with Malcolm Waterman. He's the only one in the family on the island. If he says it's okay, then I guess it's okay."

"If not," Priscilla told Katherine, "you definitely have to stay at my place. At least until you get settled somewhere else."

Once more there were tears in the old woman's eyes. "You're both too good."

"So that's it, is it?" Anna huffed. "She gets away with murder, and I get blamed for everything. We'll just see about that, Miss So-Called Waterman."

"You might want to take advantage of your right to remain silent, Ms. Vaden," April warned. "At least until you have an attorney to advise you."

"Stand up, ma'am," Rogers said to Anna.

As he put the handcuffs on Anna, April read her her rights.

"Do you think you can give me a lift back to my cousin's house?" Priscilla asked April as she and Rogers led their prisoner out of the room. "We're supposed to be out looking for a lost puppy, and after all this time, Joan and my other cousins are going to be wondering where I am."

"Yeah, sure." April looked back at Rogers and Anna. "They can sit in back for a few blocks."

"Are you both going to be all right here?" Priscilla asked Kitty and her aunt. "I don't know why Joan or Gerald hasn't called me, unless my phone died or something." She rummaged in her purse and checked her phone. "Yep. Dead as a doornail. Anyway, they're going to be worried if I don't check in with them. But I'll get my car and come back, all right?"

"We'll be just fine," Kitty said. "Aunt Katherine and I have a lot of catching up to do."

"You just stay put," April warned Katherine. "You have a lot of explaining to do to the DA and to the Waterman family."

"I understand," Katherine said. "Whatever happens next, I'm glad this is all over at last."

On the ride back to Joan's house, Priscilla told April how she and Kitty got into the house and what had happened with Anna trying to set the dog on them.

"You'll have to make a report," April said. "It would help if we had a record of everything you've done since you ran into your friend Kitty."

"I'd be glad to, and I'm sure Kitty—wait! Can you stop here?"

Priscilla thanked her and hopped out of the car as soon as it pulled over to the curb. Gerald and her cousins were coming from the direction of Joan's house.

"Where have you been?" Joan asked as the police car drove away.

"We've been calling and calling!" Trudy scolded.

"Are you all right?" Gerald asked. "We were coming to find you. Where's Kitty?"

Gail looked concerned. "Is she okay? Who was that in the squad car?"

"I can't answer everything at once," Priscilla said with a laugh. "I'm sorry, but my phone died. Kitty's back at the Waterman house, that was Miss Waterman's housekeeper being taken to jail, and I have a huge and extremely unbelievable story to tell all of you. First, though, what about Sister? Did you find her?"

Joan shook her head, looking as if she might cry again. "Nothing. We called and looked and then, when we couldn't get in touch with you, we thought we'd better try to find you and Kitty. You didn't see any sign of her out that way?"

"I'm sorry, no. We sort of got off track."

As they walked back to Joan's house, Priscilla told them as briefly as she could about Kitty's aunt and everything that had happened since Miss Waterman's death.

"So the housekeeper was blackmailing her all that time," Gerald said. "Wow."

"I'm glad your friend got a second chance to get in touch with her aunt," Gail said. "We don't always get those."

Joan started to cry, and Gail took her arm.

"It's all right. It's going to be all right."

"Sister's gone," Joan sobbed, "and I'm not going to get another chance to let her know I love her and want her."

Priscilla stopped short, making Joan stop too. "We're going to find her, okay? Just because we haven't yet, that doesn't mean we won't. We're going to keep looking as long as we need to, all right?"

Joan nodded, clearly unconvinced.

"Let's go back to your house, get something cold to drink, and figure out what to do next. Everybody all right with that?"

Joan's cottage was just around the corner, and in a few minutes they were all sitting in the living room.

"I think we should split into teams again and try some other directions," Priscilla said. "Sister's just a little thing. I can't imagine she could get very far."

"Unless something got her," Joan said, her voice thick. "Or she got out into the street, and somebody—"

She broke off, and they all turned at the sound from the back door. For a moment there was nothing, and then it came again. A soft little whine. A puppy's whine.

"Sister!"

Joan leaped up, and everyone followed her into the kitchen. She threw open the back door, and Sister trotted in, her whole body wriggling in rhythm with her wagging stub of a tail.

"Oh, sweetie!" Joan picked her up, kissing her nose and cheeks and being licked ecstatically in return. "Where have you been? Why did you go? I'm so sorry. I'm so sorry I made you think I didn't want you. I'm sorry you thought I didn't love you."

Priscilla laughed, almost crying herself to see Joan so happy to have the puppy back. "I think she just wanted to explore a bit."

"She doesn't look all that dirty," Gerald said with a grin, "or that tired. I bet she played for a while and then conked out somewhere and never heard you calling."

Joan hugged the puppy tightly, smiling through her tears. "Thank God that's all it was."

Thank You, God, Priscilla thought. *Thank You that they're both all right.*

CHAPTER NINETEEN

As soon as Joan and Sister were happily settled again, Priscilla went back to her own cottage, packed up Kitty's things and a few of her own, and then drove over to the Waterman house. She was a little surprised to see a green Acura parked out front, though she knew she shouldn't have been.

"I thought I'd stay too," she told Kitty when she answered the door. "That way you'll have all your things together and a ride to the airport bright and early."

"Oh, that would be wonderful." Kitty looked up the stairway and then lowered her voice. "Malcolm Waterman is here."

"I noticed. What does he want?"

"I guess April Brown must have told him about everything. He's upstairs talking to Aunt Katherine."

"Maybe we'd better get up there too."

They found Malcolm sitting in a straight-backed chair facing Katherine. He didn't look mad. He looked thoughtful. The German shepherd lay at their feet.

"She would have seen you," Katherine was saying. "She would have after you sent that letter telling her you were sorry and wanted to patch things up. I know she would have. She talked about you often. I think she was sorry after that girl left you. She wanted you to be happy, and she didn't want you to be hurt. But you know how proud and stubborn she could be. She wasn't going to take the first step."

His smile was a little wistful. "I know. I guess I inherited some of that too. I just wish I hadn't waited so long to try to make up with her."

"You understand why I couldn't see you, of course. You were the one who had seen her the most and the most recently. But I hated that part. I know that must have hurt you."

Seeing Priscilla and Kitty in the doorway, Malcolm stood. "Thank you for telling me everything. About what happened. I can't tell you what the rest of the family is going to do, but as far as I'm concerned, if we can get back what you gave to that Vaden woman, I guess we can call the rest square. I can't see that you spent any more of Aunt Caroline's money since she died than she would have herself if she'd lived."

Katherine smiled sadly and took his hand. "We never did live very high, Caroline and I, and I never wanted to after she was gone. Thank you for understanding."

He gave her hand a squeeze and, with a nod at Priscilla and Kitty, went down the stairs. Priscilla heard him open the door, and then she heard him talking to someone. She walked down the hallway and looked over the stair rail. The new arrival was Rowan Cavanaugh IV.

With a glance toward the back bedroom, she hurried down the stairs to the two men. "Mr. Cavanaugh. We weren't expecting you."

"I, uh, heard that Katherine Evans is still alive, and I thought I'd see if she'd speak to me for a moment or two."

He'd heard, had he? Priscilla didn't say anything, but it had to have been Anna who told him. She had been awfully sure he would take care of her if she got into any trouble. She must have called him from the police station and told him everything.

"Like I told you," Malcolm said, "I don't know anything besides what I've already told you. She didn't say anything to me about your grandmother or any of your family. She probably doesn't know anything more than I do."

With that, he slipped past Mr. Cavanaugh and down the side-walk to his car.

"Do you think she'd see me for a minute?" Mr. Cavanaugh asked once Malcolm was gone. "I really need to talk to her."

Priscilla looked him over warily. "We're not going to let you badger her. She's been through a lot since Miss Waterman died."

"I just want to ask her a few questions, that's all. In private."

"That will be up to her, whether she wants to see you at all and whether she wants to be alone with you. I'll ask her."

Mr. Cavanaugh nodded.

Priscilla went up the stairs and was back at the door a minute later. "She'll see you, but she would rather Kitty and I stayed with her. Whatever you have to tell her, you have our word we won't say anything to anyone about it."

Mr. Cavanaugh fixed his eyes on her, something a little ruthless and chilling behind them. "If a word of this gets out, I'll know where it came from."

"I realize that, but if you think you can trust Anna Vaden with whatever this is, then I think you can be at least as sure of me and Kitty." She smiled faintly. "And we won't ask anything in return."

He gave a nod and followed her up to the back bedroom. Kitty was sitting on the chaise next to Katherine now, looking equal parts anxious and protective. The lady herself sat with her frail hands clasped in her lap, head held high, gaze direct.

"You're Rowan Cavanaugh the Fourth," she said, looking the man over. "I see much of your father in you. I knew him when he was a child."

"He mentioned you too, from time to time," Mr. Cavanaugh said, taking the chair Malcolm had sat in. "He said you and my grandmother were good friends."

"We were. She was a great lady, and I won't hear anything said against her."

"Then we are agreed on that point," Mr. Cavanaugh said. He took a letter out of his pocket and handed it to her. "Have you seen this before?"

The look on Katherine's face said that she had. "This is what Anna sold you, isn't it?" she asked, not opening the envelope.

"It is. That's what brought me here."

Looking more weary than intrigued, Katherine stared at the envelope bordered with red, white, and blue. It was tanned with age, the blue ink in the address fading, the smudged postmark showing the date of February 14, 1945. It had been mailed from Martha's Vineyard and was addressed to 2nd Lt. Maxwell S. Waterman, Co. F, 394th Inf., APO #26, c/o Postmaster, New York, NY.

"Waterman?" Kitty said, staring at it. "Which Waterman was he?"

Mr. Cavanaugh's expression was tense, a little irritated.

Katherine only looked sad. "He was Caroline's brother," she said. "I never met him, of course, but I saw photographs. Tall, blond, and very good looking, especially in uniform. Caroline always said he was a real charmer."

"You've seen this before, haven't you?" Mr. Cavanaugh accused.

Katherine sighed, and the dog looked at her quizzically. "Max and Rosie Cavanaugh met when Rowan Cavanaugh—the Second, that is—married her all of a sudden and brought her home from Georgia. That was in the spring of '41. It was a whirlwind romance, and evidently she had the glamour and charisma to really put the Cavanaughs on the map with the American public. The Cavanaughs and the Watermans were still close back then, I'm told, so Rosie and Max saw each other a lot in those few months before the US entered the war."

"What happened?" Priscilla asked, almost certain she already knew.

Katherine took the letter out of the envelope. "The military sent this home with the rest of Max's things after he was killed crossing that Remagen bridge into Germany in 1945. The war was nearly over. Caroline's mother and then Caroline herself kept everything of his in a trunk upstairs. I suppose Anna must have found it when she was snooping around for something she could force me to sell to get some money for her. I never even knew it was missing."

Kitty knitted her brow. "If he was in Germany, why did Caroline send the letter to New York?"

"People in the States sent all their mail there," Katherine explained, "at least for the European Theater. The Army was responsible for shipping it overseas and getting it delivered to wherever the soldier it was addressed to was serving at the time."

"Miss Waterman showed you this?" Mr. Cavanaugh asked stiffly.

"We didn't have much to do but talk about the past forty-six years, Mr. Cavanaugh. If there's something about Caroline I don't know, I expect she didn't know it either."

Katherine unfolded the letter, brittle now with age, and Priscilla read it over her shoulder. It was written in the lovely copperplate script, flowing and feminine, that had vanished with the advent of the ballpoint pen.

Dearest Max,

I'm so glad you're not angry with me. I can't help being a little happy about it anyway. To tell the truth, I'm just dying to tell someone about us, but I know it will have to wait, as you have more important things to take care of right now. It's Valentine's Day, my dearest love, and how can I think of anyone but you? Rowan will understand. He'll have to understand. He'll have to let me go now, if he loves me even a little bit. But we'll tell him together, if you're sure, with all that's happened, that you don't want to run the other way. There won't be any way to avoid a huge scandal, but I can take it if you can. I hear things are better and better where you are and that you'll soon be coming home. I must hurry before someone asks me what I'm writing and slip this into the mail before anyone sees. I'll have a laurel wreath waiting for my hero and my only Valentine.

Yours always,

Rosie

P.S. Don't ask me to throw away your letters, darling. Every one of them is precious to me. But you know where I keep them. No one else will know they're there.

"Miss Waterman told you about him and my grandmother?" Mr. Cavanaugh asked, his face flint.

"No," Katherine admitted, "your grandmother did."

"My—"

"She told me herself." Katherine shook her head, grief and pity in her eyes. "You can't have known how it was for her." She looked at Mr. Cavanaugh for a moment, and then she shook her head again. "Or maybe you do, but you were raised that way. She wasn't. She'd been brought into the family and immediately put on display. Everything she said or did or ate or wore was immediately the talk of the town. Her husband was gone for long stretches, first in the war and then running for office and then being in office. Her own family was down South, and everyone around her always wanted something from her, money or patronage or 'just a little word in your husband's ear . . . ' Once she told me she'd give ten years of her life for just a week of peace and quiet."

Cavanaugh shrugged and said nothing.

"She realized she could confide in me, and I wasn't going to say a word to anyone. I never did. I never would have." Katherine's expression softened into understanding pity. "I know this letter looks bad, but I don't think it was more than a fantasy between her and Max. They liked each other, of course. Caroline told me there was something electric between them every time they happened to be at the same party or at dinner at the Cavanaughs' or the Watermans' or wherever they happened to meet. They never made it obvious, Caroline said, but she knew. Would Max and Rosie have actually run away together once he came home? I don't know. Maybe they would have, but the fact is that he didn't make it back. He didn't end up being anything but a fond memory, and Rosie stayed with her husband until she died."

"And there was never anyone else?" Mr. Cavanaugh asked. "Not after him?"

His voice was harsh enough to make Rex lift his head and growl very low.

"I never heard her mention anyone. Of course, I didn't know her until 1965, well after Max's death, but he was the only one she ever said anything about. And then it was only when she was sure no one would hear. I'm sure she never meant to hurt your grandfather, and after all, Max was gone."

Mr. Cavanaugh narrowed his eyes. "What about this hiding place she said she had? Did she ever mention that to you?"

Katherine nodded. "There were false bottoms in the drawers where she kept her lingerie. Not really deep enough for anyone to notice they were there."

"That antique dresser she had in her bedroom?" Mr. Cavanaugh asked.

"That's the one."

He snorted. "I tore just about everything that was hers apart once I got ahold of that letter. I was determined to get my hands on all the others. I found those false-bottomed drawers. They were empty. If Grandmother kept all his letters, where'd they go?"

Katherine sighed. "Even I didn't know about those letters until she was dying. She was terribly ill, and the doctors said she didn't have more than a few hours left, and she knew it. She had kept his letters all those years, but she couldn't risk them being found. She said what she had done was wrong, but she didn't want anything left to cause your grandfather or your father any more pain than they were already going through. She asked me to get the letters and burn them. She said she couldn't bring herself to do it while she was alive, but now there was no reason to leave them for someone else to find."

Mr. Cavanaugh's eyes were barely slits now. "And you didn't read them?"

"I did as she asked and burned them all. I never opened any of them. I didn't even count them or look at the postmark dates. They weren't my business, and she wanted them gone."

"So there's really nothing more to find." Mr. Cavanaugh looked cautiously relieved. "You don't think there's anything left that would indicate there was anything between her and this Waterman guy?"

"I promise you, upon my soul, I burned everything that was there."

"Okay, then. I guess there's nothing more to worry about. If I can keep that Vaden woman quiet, then we're all right."

"You don't have to worry about us," Kitty said earnestly. "We'd never say anything, would we, Priscilla?"

Priscilla shook her head.

"Even if this letter got out," Katherine added, "what does it really say? Just that decades ago a twenty-three-year-old girl made some foolish plans that were never realized. Apart from that, there's nothing anyone can prove or even suggest that would indicate she was anything but a faithful wife and good mother until the day she died. In this day and age, no one would even bat an eye at what's in this."

Mr. Cavanaugh exhaled. "I guess you're right. But Rosie Cavanaugh was always such a symbol of our family. People liked us because they liked her. They still like her. They're still fascinated by her, and I won't have her memory spoiled by something as tawdry as this."

"You don't have to worry," Katherine soothed. "As I told you, I burned everything hidden in the dresser. This is the only letter that was sent back with Max's things. Caroline kept it because it was the last thing she had of her brother's, but she's gone now too. If you'd feel better destroying it, I don't guess there's any reason to stop you."

Mr. Cavanaugh looked at her for a moment. Then he went to the fireplace, opened the flue, and set the letter and envelope on the grate. "You're sure?"

Katherine nodded solemnly.

He got a match from the mantelpiece, struck it, and touched it to a corner of the brittle paper. A moment later it was nothing but curling ash.

"Thank you for understanding," he said after he closed the flue again and shoveled the ashes into a nearby trash can. "You've all been very kind, and I appreciate it." He bowed formally over Katherine's hand. "I won't forget what you did for her. For all of us."

"She was my friend," the old woman said simply.

He looked at her for a long moment and then nodded slowly. "It's been an honor, ma'am."

He showed himself out, and the three women watched from the upstairs window until the black Lamborghini drove away.

"Wow," Kitty breathed. She plopped back onto the chaise next to her aunt. "What a story. Do you think he can get Anna to keep quiet about it?"

"I think your aunt is right," Priscilla said. "There's not much in that letter that proves anything but wishful thinking. A lot of what might have been. Maybe there would have been a scandal if Max had come back, but it's all just speculation. It's probably best that it ended the way it did."

She smiled at Katherine, but then her smile faded. Katherine wasn't smiling back.

"What is it?" Priscilla asked.

Katherine looked down, her expression troubled. "It's not quite as simple as that," she murmured.

Priscilla and Kitty both looked at her, waiting for her to go on. "What is it?" Priscilla urged when she said nothing.

Katherine sighed. "I'm not sure what to say. What I should do. I suppose I should burn this one too, but she asked me to keep it. She couldn't bear for everything of his to be destroyed. Not his very last one."

Kitty stared at her, round-eyed. "You have another letter."

"You swore you destroyed all of them," Priscilla said.

"I swore that I destroyed all the ones hidden in her dresser, and I did, just as I said. I burned them the day she died and flushed the ashes down the toilet."

"Then what—"

"Come with me."

With Rex at her heels, Katherine led them down the stairs to a bedroom next to the kitchen.

"This is the housekeeper's room. It was my room before Caroline died. It's been Anna's for the past two years. I knew she was looking all over the house for valuables. She had no idea how close she was all that time to the biggest payoff of her life."

It was a fairly large room, not lavish but well put together and nicely decorated. The double bed had a substantial head-board with a lighted bookshelf built in. Katherine cleared the books from one end of the lowest shelf and then fidgeted for a moment with the shelf itself. A panel slid to one side, revealing an opening that was perhaps six inches wide by eight inches long and three or four inches deep. Inside lay a small book with a delicate lace cover. With careful hands, Katherine lifted it out.

"Rosie Cavanaugh's prayer book."

CHAPTER TWENTY

Priscilla glanced at Kitty, who looked as if she didn't dare breathe.

"She had it with her in the hospital," Katherine said, running one finger along the edge of the prayer book's cover. "She gave it to me that final day. She said she knew I'd keep it to remember her and to keep it safe. That was when she told me about the last letter."

She opened the little book to the back cover and then worked her fingers behind the pink satin lining on the side nearest the binding. It took her a few seconds to wriggle out a tiny envelope.

"What's that?" Kitty asked. "A copy?"

"It's V-mail," Katherine told her, taking from the envelope an equally tiny, slick-surfaced letter. "During the war, they needed to cut down on the bulk and weight of letters being mailed back to the States from the soldiers, so they'd copy the letters on film, ship the film back home, and then print out the letters like this and mail them out." For the next minute or two, she didn't say anything. She merely held the little yellowed page, still folded, in both hands. Finally she opened it and handed it to Kitty. "It's too small for me to read anymore."

Kitty opened it and began to read, but Katherine stopped her.

"Would you mind reading it aloud? It's been a very, very long time since I looked at it, and I want to make sure I'm remembering it right."

"All right," Kitty said softly, and then she cleared her throat. "It's dated March 6, 1945. 'Lover, how can you think I could ever hate you? I'm still wondering what your husband will say. You'd better let me tell him once I come home. Schicklgruber—'" Her forehead wrinkled at the name, but she kept on. "'Schicklgruber is about licked, from what I can tell. We're heading right for—'" She frowned. "Part of it's blacked out."

Katherine nodded. "They would have censored anything that gave any kind of information about where he was or what he was doing. Caroline was sure that must have said Berlin or at least Germany, since they told her family where he was killed."

"Okay," Kitty said, and she began to read again. "'We're heading right for *blank* now, and the Nutsies know they can't stop us. Until I can take care of you both, you take care of our little one.'"

She broke off, eyes wide, and Katherine urged her to continue.

"'I can't quite believe it still,'" Kitty read, steadying her voice, "'but I'm not sorry. How could I not want the kid if you're its mother? Anyway, they're rounding up the mail, so I have to quit for now. Know I'll stand by you, whatever happens. Love you more than ever and then some. Max.'"

There was silence for a moment, and then Kitty looked up from the paper. "A baby."

"I'm not going to make excuses for what they did," Katherine said wearily. "She knew it was wrong, and she tried all the rest of her life to make sure her husband never knew, but she kept that one letter, Max's very last, there in her prayer book to remind her of the wrong she'd done, to remind her to pray for God's mercy and forgiveness for them both."

"But the baby," Priscilla said. "She didn't—"

"The baby was born on August 15, 1945, the same day the Japanese surrendered." Katherine smiled faintly. "They named him Rowan Cavanaugh the Third."

Priscilla couldn't think of a thing to say. Rowan Cavanaugh III wasn't a Cavanaugh at all. And that meant neither was Rowan Cavanaugh IV.

"She was fortunate that the boy looked like her and not like Max," Katherine said.

"But don't you think he should know now?" Kitty asked, handing the letter back to her. "Mr. Cavanaugh, I mean."

"What good would that do? It wasn't that child's fault. Or the child's child's. Or anyone after him. Rosie and her husband didn't have any other children. The child she and Max had was raised as a Cavanaugh. If he had been adopted by them, he would have had all the rights of a natural-born child. And, as far as the law is concerned, any child born during a marriage is legally the husband's child anyway. What good would it do to bring all of this out now? It wouldn't benefit anyone. It would only cause a lot of pain."

She was right. No good would come from making this known, even to Cavanaugh privately. Being a Cavanaugh was all he had ever known, and he was obviously protective of the name. That had been clear when he believed Anna had uncovered proof of his grandmother's affair. Telling him what was in Max's last letter would be needlessly cruel.

"But why did you tell us?" Priscilla asked. "Why not just destroy the book and the letter? Then no one else would have ever known."

"I couldn't." There was a tiny quaver in Katherine's voice. "She trusted me with them, and it was all that was left of her and her love for Max. I can't destroy them. I promised her I'd keep them safe."

"But you let Mr. Cavanaugh burn Rosie's letter," Priscilla said.

There was a touch of pain in Katherine's expression. "I hated that, but I wanted him to know for certain that the letter was gone and could never resurface. He deserved that much."

"That hiding place in the headboard," Kitty said. "How did you arrange for that?"

"That was Caroline's doing. We were talking about Max. Max had written to her once, telling her about him and Rosie. She destroyed that letter the minute she read it, and didn't tell anyone what he had said. When she told me about it, I told her about the prayer book and the letter inside. I told her I was worried it would be found someday. She had the headboard made and moved into my room, oh, I don't remember now—twenty or twenty-five years ago, I think. I told her she ought to put Rosie's letter to Max in there too. But she said with only the two of us living in the house, she wasn't worried about it, that she trusted me to destroy it after she was gone. The way she went..." Katherine bit her lip. "It was so sudden, I never even thought of that letter. Not until I heard Rowan Cavanaugh was nosing around for information about his grandmother. By then, it was much too late to do anything about it."

She put the other letter, Max's letter, back into its envelope and tucked it into the lining of the prayer book once more. For a moment, she sat with the book clasped in her hands, staring at it but obviously seeing something long past.

Then she pressed the book into Kitty's hands. "There's really no one else I can trust with this."

Kitty gaped at her. "But—"

"I don't know what's going to happen to me once all this mess I'm in has been straightened out, but I don't want anyone else finding this. I don't want what's in there coming out once I've passed on. I want you to take it home with you and put it away somewhere safe. And when I'm gone, you destroy it all. Then I'll have kept my promise to Rosie Cavanaugh, and nobody will be hurt because of it."

For a moment, Kitty looked uncertain. Then she clasped the book against her chest. "I'll take care of it, Aunt Katherine. I promise. It'll be safe until you're gone, and then I'll make sure it's all destroyed."

Katherine's lined lips trembled into a smile. "You must think me a sentimental old fool to make such a fuss over a book and an old letter, but I couldn't go back on a promise. To either of them."

Kitty hugged her, eyes shining.

"I think they were both lucky to have you for a friend," Priscilla said. "Rosie Cavanaugh and Caroline Waterman."

"They were both good to me, especially after my second husband died and I was out here with no family and no money. I was happy to do what I could to look after them both."

Kitty looked at the book again, and there was a sudden pensiveness in her expression. "I wish I could stay longer, but I've stayed too long as it is, and too many people are depending on me to get this deal done."

"I understand, honey, and it's all right." Katherine patted her knee. "You just go and do whatever it is you need to do. That girl with the police seems very nice, and I'm sure she'll see I get a fair shake."

"I'm not going to let you go through all this by yourself," Priscilla assured her. "If the Watermans want you to leave the house, then you can stay with me until you decide what you want to do. I think Kitty can vouch for my guest room."

"You'll certainly be comfortable there," Kitty said. "And Priscilla has lots of good movies."

"Oh no, Priscilla honey, I couldn't do that. It's too good of you, but I'd have Rex, you see, and I can't abandon him now." The dog lifted his head at the sound of his name, and Katherine patted him. "You have a dog, don't you? I wouldn't want him to be upset by a stranger coming to stay."

Just then Priscilla had a terrible thought, but before she could push it aside, Kitty said it aloud.

"But he's Anna's dog, isn't he? I mean, legally? What if she—" Kitty bit her lip. "What if she wants him back?"

Katherine laid her hand on the dog's head. "But she doesn't care anything about him. She was only using him to intimidate me and anyone else who might come around. Surely she wouldn't cause any trouble over him."

"She's exactly the type to do precisely that," Priscilla said, her mouth tight. "Just for spite."

"That's not right," Katherine said, pulling the dog's head over against her leg, petting him still. "Poor Rex. It's not right."

"I think I might have some ideas for what to do about him," Priscilla said, "but why don't you let me worry about that for now? In the meantime, there's not a lot any of us can do about any of this, so why don't we find someplace comfortable where we can sit and talk? I know you and Kitty will want to catch up on everything you've both been up to since she was a little girl."

Katherine took Priscilla's and Kitty's arms. "I think with both of you on my side, this will all work out somehow."

They spent the rest of the day talking, catching up, and getting better acquainted.

"You don't know how nice it is to have someone to talk to again," Katherine said as they sat down to the dinner Kitty and Priscilla had put together, a touch of pink in her softly lined cheeks. "I'm going to hate for you to go, Kitty."

"I'm going to hate to leave now," Kitty told her. "Are you sure you shouldn't just come home with me tomorrow? I already talked to Keith about it. He wouldn't mind at all. At least until you have a place of your own."

"They won't let me, will they?" Katherine asked. "The police, I mean. Won't they want me to be here to stand trial or whatever must happen?"

"I hope it won't have to go as far as that," Priscilla said. "I'm sure they'll want you to testify against Anna, but that will probably take months to resolve."

"I don't want to press charges against her." There was a determined set to Katherine's mouth. "I'll testify about the blackmail if I have to in order to get the Watermans their money back, but I don't want to press charges about everything else. I got myself into this mess, and if Malcolm and his family are going to go easy on me, I don't think I could do any less for Anna."

"The difference is that you didn't mean any harm in what you did," Priscilla said. "She definitely did."

"You wouldn't want her blackmailing someone else," Kitty added.

"The police know about her now," Katherine said. "And she really is just a big coward. I don't think she would have had the nerve to do what she did if she hadn't just happened onto my situation, where she knew I was totally powerless."

Priscilla's concerned expression softened. "I guess we all deserve a second chance, though I couldn't tell that she was the least bit sorry for what she did."

"She was sorry she got caught," Kitty said.

"Well, we'll see what happens now." Katherine smiled. "You don't know how good it feels to just be Katherine Evans again, to have all this out in the open, to not have to worry about being caught. It's just...good."

Katherine went with Priscilla to take Kitty to the airport the next morning.

"You make sure and call me as soon as you find out what the district attorney says." Kitty hugged her aunt tightly as they approached the security checkpoint. "And you think about coming to stay with me and Keith. We'd love to have you, and I'm sure we could find you a little place close to us where you could settle permanently."

"We'll see, honey." Katherine kissed her on both cheeks. "I'll certainly write you."

"And call!" Kitty insisted.

"And call."

"You keep in touch with me too," Priscilla insisted, hugging Kitty as well.

"I will. I'd better go or I won't make it to my gate in time!"

Kitty grabbed her carry-on and, with a little wave, hurried to the line and was gone.

Katherine dabbed her eyes with a dainty little handkerchief and then smiled. "What now?"

"Now I think we need to see if Mr. Edison has a minute to visit with us."

They drove to the attorney's office, and after only a few minutes' wait, he was able to see them. Katherine's story took him very much by surprise, but once it was told, Edison became rather protective of her. Since he would be representing Caroline Waterman's estate in the probate of her will and in the recovery of the assets that had been paid over to Anna Vaden, he didn't feel it was ethical to represent Katherine too, but he did refer her to another attorney whose office was only two blocks away.

"He'll see to everything for you. Just tell him I sent you over. And as far as that other matter we discussed, Mrs. Grant, my secretary is working on it right now. It won't take more than a few minutes."

Fifteen minutes later, Priscilla and Katherine were on their way to talk to April Brown at the police station.

"I discussed all this with the district attorney yesterday, Mrs. Evans," April said. "He couldn't make me any guarantees, and he said a lot of what happens will depend on what the Watermans say and how cooperative Anna Vaden is about returning all the money you gave her."

"Will it encourage her to cooperate if she knows, provided she *does* cooperate, that none of us want to press charges against her?" Priscilla asked.

"It might," April said. "The more of these things we can settle out of court, the better."

"I'm not planning on fighting any of this," Katherine said quietly. "I'm guilty."

"I think, given the circumstances, people are going to understand why you did what you did, but again, it's going to take some time to untangle all of this. Do you have an attorney?"

Katherine glanced at Priscilla. "I've been referred to one."

"Good. If you find out he or she is going to be more than you can afford, let me know. We'll have the court appoint one for you."

Katherine nodded meekly, but there was a touch of worry in her eyes. She didn't have a cent of her own to pay anyone for legal help.

Priscilla gave her hand a comforting squeeze. "We'll work it out, whatever it is." Then she handed April the paper she had gotten from Mr. Edison. "Do you think she'll sign?"

April read it over, suppressed a little grin, and stood up. "I'll go find out."

She was back a few minutes later. Smiling, she sat behind her desk again and passed the folded paper over to Katherine.

"Did she—?" Katherine unfolded the paper, and her eyes lit up. "Oh, thank God. Thank you. Thank you so much."

Priscilla looked the paper over. It gave Katherine Evans all rights to the German shepherd known as Rex and was signed by Anna Vaden, witnessed by April Brown and another officer, Ed Sequeira.

"I feel so much better about him now," Katherine said, giving April's arm a grateful squeeze. "Thank you. I know you have to do your job, but thank you for being so understanding about all this."

"That's part of my job too, Mrs. Evans," April said, smiling. "You go on home and don't worry about this for now. We'll be in touch with you."

"Thank you," Katherine repeated as she stood.

"Remember," April added, "if you go anywhere, you let us know how we can reach you, okay?"

"I'll remember."

"I'm so happy Anna didn't give you any trouble about the dog," Priscilla said once she and Katherine were driving away from the police station.

"I am too. Now I just have to figure out where I'm going to sleep tonight."

"What do you mean?" Priscilla asked. "At your house, of course."

"Miss Waterman's house, you mean. I can't just stay there and wait for her family to throw me out."

"Surely they wouldn't do that, would they? At least not right away."

Katherine pursed her lined lips, thinking for a long moment. "I'd sure like to have a little talk with Malcolm Waterman."

"I suppose we could do that. As long as you're not too tired after all the running around we've already done today."

Katherine chuckled. "I'm not so old that I need naps, young lady. Not quite yet. Now, you don't happen to know where Malcolm lives, do you?"

"I do. But if you don't mind, before we go there, I'd like to give my cousin a quick call, just to see how she's doing. She and her new puppy."

Katherine smiled. "Good idea."

Priscilla pulled over at her first opportunity and dialed the phone.

"Hello?" Joan whispered.

"Joan?" Priscilla said. "Is that you? Are you okay?"

Joan's laugh was very soft. "Everything's fine. I just have a sleeping puppy in my lap, and I don't want to wake her. I had my ringtone turned down to almost nothing, so I'm glad I noticed you were calling. What's going on?"

Priscilla couldn't possibly have smiled any wider. "Aww, how are things going with Sister?"

"They couldn't be better. I'm sorry it took me so long to realize how much I need her and what a sweetie she is. And I've realized something else too."

"What's that?" Priscilla asked.

"That my Kansas cousin is pretty smart."

Priscilla laughed. "I'm glad the two of you are getting along now."

"That doesn't mean she didn't chew up my shoe and the magazine I just got." There was more than a touch of indulgent fondness in Joan's whisper. "But puppies will be puppies."

"I knew you were just perfect for each other."

"What are you up to?" Joan whispered.

"We just dropped Kitty off at the airport and then visited Miss Waterman's lawyer." Priscilla told her what had happened at the police station, especially about Rex. "And now Katherine wants to talk to Malcolm, so we're going to go over to his place and see if he's in."

"Good luck," Joan said softly. "Let me know how it goes."

Malcolm looked startled when he opened his front door. "Well, this is pretty convenient. I was about to see if I could come talk to you, Mrs. Evans. Would you like to come in?"

"That would be very nice of you," Katherine said, and she and Priscilla followed him inside.

Despite her earlier protestations, when Katherine was finally settled on Malcolm's couch, she looked exhausted. Or perhaps, Priscilla considered, it was uncertainty that made her lips tremble.

"You were coming to see us?" Priscilla prompted when Malcolm didn't speak up.

"Uh, yeah," he said. "I talked to my sisters about everything that happened, Mrs. Evans. Donna, my oldest sister, was pretty mad at first and said we ought to press charges, but when I'd told them everything, she changed her mind. We're all pretty ashamed of how we treated Aunt Caroline, ignoring her all these years, and that you got tangled up in the middle of it. We figure the least we can do is let you stay in the house until you find a place to live."

"Thank you," Katherine said. "And thank them for me. I don't know where I'll go or what I'll do, but I'll try not to stay too long."

"You take your time," he said. "As I told my sisters, we're all going to be pretty well off with everything we'll inherit from Aunt Caroline. There's no reason we can't help you get settled somewhere too."

There wasn't much more to talk about after that, and they left Malcolm's house a few minutes later. Katherine was silent as they drove away.

"Tired?" Priscilla asked.

Katherine shook her head but didn't say anything.

"He and the rest of the family are being pretty nice about everything, don't you think?" Priscilla added.

"They are," Katherine said, her voice rather thin. "I just don't know what I'm going to do about any of this. I don't have any money to speak of. I don't have a car or even a driver's license anymore. I had to let mine expire a year and a half ago. I don't even exist as far as the authorities are concerned. What am I going to do?"

"You're not going to worry, okay? We'll see to things one at a time, and trust God to provide for you. Don't you think He knows what you need?"

She nodded, smiling a little. "I just don't know how He's going to get it to me."

Priscilla smiled too. "Let Him worry about that, okay? For now, we'd better stop by my place so I can let my dog out, and then we'll go back to your house and do some planning. Maybe you and Rex and I will watch a movie or two while we're at it. How does that sound?"

"Good," Katherine said. "Very, very good."

It wasn't long before they were at the Waterman house again. Priscilla looked it over as they walked from the car to the front door. It was a big place, far too large for Katherine to stay there alone for much longer. It had been her home for almost fifty years, but most recently it had been more of a prison than a home. It would be good for her to have a place of her own, a cozy little place for her and Rex. Maybe she'd take Kitty up on her offer and move out to the West Coast.

"What's that?" Katherine asked when they stepped onto the porch.

There was a package, a foot-long rectangle wrapped in white paper, propped up against the front door. Leaning against it was an envelope. The only thing written on it was *Mrs. Evans.*

Priscilla picked up the envelope and the package and followed Katherine inside. Rex greeted them tentatively but seemed happy to have company again. Priscilla fed him and let him outside, and then she sat down on the living room sofa next to Katherine.

"Well?" she asked, looking at the still-unopened package.

"Should I?" Katherine asked her. "I wasn't expecting anything, you know."

"It's addressed to you. I think you have every right to open it."

There was an uncertain little pucker in the older woman's forehead, but she slid one withered finger under the flap of the envelope and took out the paper that was inside. When she unfolded it, she caught a startled breath. "Oh my."

"What?" Priscilla asked, leaning over to see for herself, and her own eyes widened. "Cavanaugh? What in the world?"

"Let me read it," Katherine said. "'My dear Mrs. Evans, please allow me to thank you for your kindness and understanding in the matter we discussed recently. You don't realize how upset I have been, wondering how this situation could end in a manner that would not be damaging to so many people. You have certainly set my mind at ease, not only regarding the disposal of the information itself, but in helping me to see that it was nothing I need have worried myself about in the first place. You were in a position to tell me what I could have found out in no other way, and for that I am eternally grateful. Please accept this as a token of my appreciation for your assistance and for your loyalty to my family. If I can ever be of assistance to you in the future, please do not hesitate to call upon me. Sincerely, Rowan Cavanaugh the Fourth.'"

"Well, he certainly says a lot without saying anything," Priscilla said.

"I suppose he wants to be extra careful in case someone besides us reads it."

"What about the package?" Priscilla raised her eyebrows. "It looks like chocolates."

"Ooh, I hope so."

Katherine pulled away the paper and lifted the lid from the box. Then her mouth dropped open. Inside were several banded stacks of hundred dollar bills.

For a moment she sat there, stunned, and then she started to laugh. "I guess he knew that, until I can be declared alive again, I wouldn't be able to cash a check."

Priscilla laughed too. She had no idea how much money was there, but it would at least give Katherine a chance to start over again.

There is nothing hidden that shall not be known, Priscilla thought as Katherine began to count her unexpected windfall, *but the time at which those things become known is up to God. It is His glory too, to conceal a thing, a thing that can only hurt and not help.*

It was a genuine miracle. It seemed that God delighted in handing out His blessings in most unexpected ways. Then again, Katherine had been a blessing too, one that Mr. Cavanaugh no doubt felt was worth every penny, even though he would never really know how much.

AUTHOR LETTER

Dear Reader,

As a lifelong resident of landlocked North Texas, the idea of living on an island surrounded by ocean waters has always intrigued me. What a treat it has been for me to "visit" Martha's Vineyard during the writing of this book and to spend time with Priscilla and her cousins. Though I could never see myself leaving my home state, the idea of living right alongside them all in a little cottage with the salt wind off the sea and the rolling sound of the waves always around me is certainly appealing.

The plots for my books always begin with a "what if," and I enjoyed building this story around reclusive Miss Waterman and her unique situation. It is very true that hidden things eventually come to light, but it's also true that, as Priscilla discovered, they may not look the way anyone expected when they do. And often God, in His wisdom, keeps things hidden that would otherwise cause irreparable harm.

Besides having fun putting together this mystery, I really enjoyed giving Joan her new dog, Sister. Sister was a precious little puppy that I found online through a shelter website. I knew the minute I saw her that she was the one I had to have in my story. I knew she was perfect for Joan. I was delighted to know that, in real life, she was claimed by her forever family only an hour or so after I saw her. After I got a peek at her darling photo, I knew she wouldn't be homeless for long. I am so grateful for people who adopt abandoned, abused, and neglected dogs, cats, and other pets. All of my fur babies come from shelters, and there isn't a better, more grateful, or more loving companion in the world than a rescue animal. It's the only love money can buy.

I hope you enjoyed *Thicker Than Water* and that you'll come back to Martha's Vineyard to find out what new adventures await Priscilla and her friends.

DeAnna Julie Dodson

P. S. Many thanks to Susan Downs for inviting me to write for Guideposts and to sweet Nancy Mehl for making the introduction. God bless you both more than you could think or ask.

ABOUT THE AUTHOR

DeANNA JULIE DODSON has always been an avid reader and a lover of storytelling, whether on the page, the screen, or the stage. This, along with her keen interest in history and her Christian faith, show in her tales of love, forgiveness, and triumph over adversity. A fifth-generation Texan, she makes her home north of Dallas with three spoiled cats and, when not writing, spends her free time quilting, cross-stitching, and watching NHL hockey. Her first novels were a trilogy of medieval romances (*In Honor Bound, By Love Redeemed,* and *To Grace Surrendered*) for Crossway Books, and she has since written a number of contemporary mysteries and has plans for many more. Also, as Julianna Deering, she writes the Drew Farthering mysteries set in 1930s England. The series debuted from Bethany House with *Rules of Murder* (2013) and is followed by *Death by the Book* and *Murder at the Mikado* (2014), *Dressed for Death* (2016), and *Murder on the Moor* and *Death at Thorburn Hall* (2017). She is represented by Wendy Lawton of the Books & Such Literary Agency (www.booksandsuch.biz). Visit her website at www.deannajuliedodson.com.

AN ARMCHAIR TOUR OF MARTHA'S VINEYARD

The Flying Horses Carousel

There's a Carousel in Oak Bluffs town,
The horses don't go up or down,
The horses just go 'round and 'round,
On the Carousel in Oak Bluffs town.

I was glad to be able to arrange for Priscilla to visit the Flying Horses Carousel in Oak Bluffs. The oldest operating platform carousel in the United States, it was built in 1876 by Charles Dare and has since been designated by the US Department of the Interior as a national landmark.

It started out on Coney Island in New York and was moved to Oak Bluffs in 1884, where it has been in operation ever since. In 1986, at the grand age of 110, it was acquired by the Preservation Trust and restored. Carousel conservator Rosa Regan refurbished each of the horses individually, giving them glossy coats of bright paint and real horsehair tails and manes to go with their original oxide eyes.

Today children of all ages can ride the horses as they listen to the music of the 1923 Wurlitzer band organ and try to catch the brass ring to win a free ride.

SOMETHING DELICIOUS FROM OUR SEASIDE FRIENDS

Joan's Favorite Roasted Pears

2 tablespoons unsalted
butter (plus a little more
for the pan)
3 small ripe pears, peeled,
cored, and halved

2 tablespoons honey
¼ teaspoon ground
cardamom
a dash of salt

Heat the oven to 450 degrees. Lightly butter a shallow baking dish and arrange the pear halves inside with the cut side up. Add a pinch of salt to each pear.

Melt 2 tablespoons butter over medium-low heat. Add honey, cardamom, and another pinch of salt. Stir until the mixture is warm. Brush the tops of the pears with some of the honey butter.

Bake the pears for 10 minutes and then baste again with some of the honey butter. (If the honey butter has congealed in the pan, re-warm it.) Bake the pears for 10 minutes more.

Carefully turn the pears over, baste again with some of the honey butter and some of the pan drippings. Cook for 15 to

20 minutes longer, basting after 5 minutes and then basting again every 2 or 3 minutes after that, making sure to brush the bottom and edges of the pan to prevent burning. If the drippings are getting too dark, add 1 to 2 tablespoons of hot water and brush the pan juices again.

Cook until the pears brown all over and are caramelized around the edges. Let them cool for 5 to 10 minutes in the pan and then put them on a plate. Keep them well covered and refrigerated until eaten.

Delicious with ice cream or whipped cream. Makes 6 roasted pear halves.

Read on for a sneak peek of another exciting book
in the series Mysteries of Martha's Vineyard!

Swept Away
by Ruth Logan Herne

There it was, rising up in the distance! The lighthouse. *My lighthouse*, Priscilla Latham Grant thought anew as she drove past another gated mansion. She'd made this same drive ten months before, a trifle tentative then, but today was different.

Her farm in Kansas had been sold. The estate sale her daughter helped arrange had gone off well with a mix of laughter and tears. And Rachel was coming to spend a three-week vacation in the Vineyard, a perfect time for mother and daughter to reconnect after life's erratic twists and turns.

Priscilla pulled into her driveway, satisfied.

She'd come east from Kansas last July with more than a few misgivings. Those were gone now. Oh, she would always miss the life she had with her husband, Gary, and Rachel, but when God changed a course, it was just that: changed.

Home.

She climbed out of the car, glad to be back. Glad to be home. She took a deep breath as a soft woof drew her attention to the cottage. She crossed the drive and opened the door to the best doggie greeting ever. Jake, a stray she'd saved the year before, greeted her happily, his red tail flagging the air with excitement. And then, when she gave the right hand signal, Jake raced across the yard to make sure all was calm. All was good.

She glanced around, satisfied. She'd survived squalls, power outages, and winds that rivaled some of the toughest storms tornado alley ever offered. She'd walked away from the chronic silence of Kansas farm widowhood last July and embraced life on Martha's Vineyard during a season that was anything but quiet. Life had taken an abrupt turn when she lost Gary, and then another when Aunt Marjorie left the family home to her estranged niece. Now, nearly fifty-nine years old, Priscilla had officially closed the former chapter.

A bark drew her attention to the shore. She whistled lightly across the greening grasses waving along the ridge. To her left lay Vineyard Haven Harbor. On her right stretched the Sound. The Woods Hole ferry was approaching, en route to Vineyard Haven. Three woofs replied from up the beach, just before her red and white Aussie shepherd came streaking her way.

Jake didn't climb the steps leading up to the historic Misty Harbor lighthouse from the water below. He bounded up, filled with young doggie enthusiasm. He raced her way, wanting to leap and jump, but Priscilla put up one hand and gave a quiet command. "Off."

She read the internal struggle in the dog's eyes, but he listened, and that earned him praise as her phone rang. Her cousin Joan's number showed in the display, and she answered quickly.

"Joan, hello! Thank you so much for taking care of Jake while I was gone. It was wonderful finding him here when I pulled into the drive just now. And now that I'm back, I'm ready to get this yard in shape before the Misty Harbor tours begin. Do you have time to take a drive to the nursery this afternoon?"

Joan had a keen eye for plant placement. Between her advice and the industry of a wonderful Tisbury woman, Ida Lee Jones, the lighthouse's long-neglected gardens would bloom more proudly this year.

"Priscilla, I love blooms and blossoms as much as the next person, but our trip might have to wait." Joan paused to catch her breath, and calm, level-headed Joan never had to pause to catch her breath. "The mayor's called a surprise town meeting tonight, with almost no notice, about something even more serious than flowers."

Obviously Mayor Whipple didn't understand the importance of everblooming vs. floribunda when it came to climbing roses. "What can be more important than the earth-shaking options of my gardens?"

"Hollywood."

Joan's reply made absolutely no sense. "Now I'm just more confused." Priscilla patted her leg as she moved toward the light-keeper's cottage. Jake trotted along, happy to be home. Happy to be with her. "What's Hollywood got to do with anything?"

"There's a production company putting in an application to film later this summer."

"Isn't that kind of exciting?" Priscilla asked. She'd come east from the heart of Kansas. Not much got filmed about Kansas since *The Wizard of Oz*, and that was a long, long time ago.

"It's a nuisance," Joan assured her. "You were here last summer. You know how busy and crowded it is. Now picture it being that busy and crowded with streets shut down, beaches closed, and attractions off-limits because of a film-shooting schedule."

Joan was right. Martha's Vineyard thrummed with people from May through October, and late summer would be the very worst possible time for this kind of interruption. Even a newcomer like Priscilla could see that. "Are you free right now?"

"Free and annoyed."

"Let's meet up."

"My house or yours?"

Priscilla laughed out loud. "In Vineyard Haven, of course." Vineyard Haven was the quaint and busy village in the heart of Tisbury. "If the village and all of Tisbury are in a fuss over this, I want to be in the thick of it! You never know what odd tidbits might come our way, and they've got an iced caramel coffee at the café I've been dying to try."

"So we can stroll about and catch the drift?"

That was exactly what Priscilla wanted to do. "Yes. After over fifty years of living a quieter-than-quiet life, the thought of another Vineyard tizzy has grabbed my interest."

"Well, there will be no mysteries about this," Joan assured her. "The whole thing will be absolutely annoying, intrusive, and bothersome. Totally predictable on all counts."

"Unless you've never dealt with such a thing, like me," Priscilla reminded her. "Bear with me while I reap the benefits of a full island experience. We newcomers are likely to get a kick out of this. Until it gets in my way, of course. I'll meet you at the café in fifteen minutes. Wear your walking shoes."

"Will do," Joan promised. "Maybe I can walk off some of my angst before this meeting tonight."

Joan and angst were the opposite of synonymous. Joan was Priscilla's even-tempered, pragmatic cousin, the one who handled everything that came her way with an enviable calm. It took a lot to get Joan riled up, which meant Hollywood and the mayor better be on their guard.

Priscilla tucked Jake inside, changed into good walking shoes, and was just about to back up her car when a familiar Coast Guard SUV pulled into the drive. She put the car into Park and waited as Captain Gerald O'Bannon headed her way.

He leaned up against the driver's door and tipped his cap back just enough for her to catch the warmth in his hazel eyes. "Heading out?"

She made a face at him, then swept her running car a glance. "Possibly a question that didn't need to be asked."

He laughed, then changed the question. "I should have asked if you're heading into town. There's a meeting called for six thirty, and it should be an interesting one. I figured our resident crime-solving expert might not want to miss it. But I mostly stopped by to say welcome home. I missed you."

His smile. His words. And more than the spoken word, his gentle tone made her return more special. She stayed pragmatic on purpose, and it took a little work to do so. "Joan just filled me in," she told him. "And I have to say I like being considered an expert, but I don't think there's going to be much of a mystery involved with a Hollywood film crew making an annoyance of themselves. Although I was hoping we could get this first summer season offering lighthouse tours to go off without a hitch. I suppose that will depend on where they want to film, but the lighthouse is a draw. Still, not much mystery in that, my friend."

He didn't look convinced and leaned closer. "There is if you figure in an armored car robbery worth over three million dollars, a missing child who disappeared without a trace, and a major hurricane taking direct aim at the island."

She couldn't have taken her eyes off Gerald if she tried, and she didn't try. "When did this happen? Is this a real thing, Gerald? Part of island history?"

"Nineteen ninety-one," he told her. "August. Hurricane Bob. That's why they want to film midsummer, because the trees and the flowers will all look like they should. It was huge news, and this kind of thing is going to get the whole pot stirring again. I can't say I'm happy about that. Sometimes it's better to leave the past undisturbed."

Three million dollars. A missing child. And a hurricane? She made a skeptical face. "You're teasing me. There's no way all of that could happen at once. It's basically unbelievable."

He did a little face scrunch that always made her smile. "Suit yourself, but it happened. Either a lucky twist of fate for the robbers, or they were uniquely schooled in their skill set. In any case they got away with it, the hurricane did major damage to the island, and no one ever found out what happened to the little girl."

Instant sympathy rose. "Gerald, I can't even imagine how hard that must have been, to have a child go missing in a storm like that. And never found." She put a hand to her aching throat. "How did her parents bear it?"

"I don't know. Her mother still lives somewhere on the island. No father that I remember being mentioned, but it was long before my time. Still, it makes you think hard about things, and to have a Hollywood production company making a movie about it, bringing it all back up—"

"When nothing was solved?"

He nodded. "Incidentals like facts rarely stop Hollywood. They're calling it 'fiction based in fact' because no one knows the true story. I don't see much sense in stirring up an old case with so many loose ends, but no one's asking my opinion. And with two kids of my own, I can't imagine how this must make that mother feel."

"Which only makes them seem more shortsighted," she agreed. She motioned to the clock on the dash. "I've got to run. I'm meeting Joan, but I'm glad you filled me in on the background. Although I expect I'll hear it again in a few minutes. Joan was puffing steam on the phone."

"The locals will be buzzing." He straightened and took a big step back.

"Are you coming to the meeting?"

He shook his head. "I'm on duty. The police chief will fill me in. Are we still on for the morning stroll at the dog park?"

"Wouldn't miss it."

He smiled then, as if walking dogs together meant something more than walking dogs together. "See you at ten."

"I'll be there!"

She drove toward town, smiling. She'd come to cherish Gerald's friendship over the past year.

Oh, she wasn't foolish. Was she?

Most likely he stopped by lots of places to chat throughout his patrols, and yet...

She liked that he swung into her drive on a regular basis. No need to examine that further, not now. But it made her happy, and that was special enough for the moment.

Sign up for the
Guideposts Fiction Newsletter
and stay up-to-date on the books you love!

You'll get sneak peeks of new releases, recommendations from other Guideposts readers, and special offers just for you . . .
and it's FREE!

Just go to Guideposts.org/Newsletters today to sign up.

Find more inspiring fiction in these best-loved Guideposts series!

Mysteries of Martha's Vineyard

Come to the shores of this quaint and historic island and dig into a cozy mystery. When a recent widow inherits a lighthouse just off the coast of Massachusetts, she finds exciting adventures, new friends, and renewed hope.

Tearoom Mysteries

Mix one stately Victorian home, a charming lakeside town in Maine, and two adventurous cousins with a passion for tea and hospitality. Add a large scoop of intriguing mystery and sprinkle generously with faith, family, and friends, and you have the recipe for Tearoom Mysteries.

Sugarcreek Amish Mysteries

Be intrigued by the suspense and joyful "aha!" moments in these delightful stories. Each book in the series brings together two women of vastly different backgrounds and traditions, who realize there's much more to the "simple life" than meets the eye.

Mysteries of Silver Peak

Escape to the historic mining town of Silver Peak, Colorado, and discover how one woman's love of antiques helps her solve mysteries buried deep in the town's checkered past.

Patchwork Mysteries

Discover that life's little mysteries often have a common thread in a series where every novel contains an intriguing whodunit centered around a quilt located in a beautiful New England town.

To learn more about these books, visit Guideposts.org/Shop